THE AUTHOR

Jenna Lee Joyce is a pen name for two
friends who live eight blocks apart in
Columbus, Ohio. They have collaborated
on sixteen romances and can't conceive of
a time when they'll stop working together.
They say with a chuckle, "We've worn
such a path between our two houses, the
city may start assessing us for street
improvements!"

Wintersfield is their first Harlequin
Temptation.

"You're a very dangerous lady, Melissa."

Those were the last words Travis spoke before pulling her naked body against his.

Melissa was lost, aware of nothing but the power Travis exuded.... She responded on the most primitive level, twisting beneath him as he urged her surrender with his mouth, his hands and the intimate probings of his tongue.

"Oh, Lissa," Travis groaned. "It's hell to want a woman as much as I want you. And I'm going to do something about it—right now!"

Wintersfield

JENNA LEE JOYCE

Harlequin Books

TORONTO • NEW YORK • LONDON
AMSTERDAM • PARIS • SYDNEY • HAMBURG
STOCKHOLM • ATHENS • TOKYO • MILAN

Wintersfield was conceived because of the farming backgrounds in both authors' lives. Although few people think the life of a farmer romantic, we wanted to show that romance exists everywhere. We dedicate this book to all our farming relatives, living and dead, who provided so much material for our story. Writing the book was like re-establishing our own roots in rural America and we did so with pride. Daniel Webster once said, "When tillage begins, other arts follow. The farmers therefore are the founders of human civilization." We couldn't agree more.

———————————◆———————————

Published December 1984

ISBN 0-373-25139-4

Printed in Canada

1

THE TRACK SURROUNDING THE CORNFIELD was muddy, the deepest ruts half filled with water from a recent rain. Startled birds flew into the warm spring air when a snorting diesel tractor passed by their grove of trees. The noisy red vehicle dipped precariously from side to side as its sixteen-inch wheels challenged the mucky potholes.

"Atta girl, Rosie," Melissa Lindstrand declared fondly, patting the tractor's splattered dash before shifting into a higher gear. "Don't get us mired, and I'll buy you that beautiful soft leather seat you know I deserve."

Adjusting her bottom on the bruisingly hard steel seat, Melissa prepared herself for the next rut in the track, laughing out loud as the valiant tractor coughed with exertion, then surged through the thick sticky mud. "I knew an appeal to your vanity would get results," Melissa pronounced happily. "Keep it up, old girl. I want to get the whole north forty acres done by noon."

At the edge of the field, Melissa braked and stopped. She leaned over the steering wheel and surveyed the gently rolling landscape in front of her. Off in the distance a lush green meadow gave way to a majestic stand of oak, elm and cottonwood. Calico

Creek meandered through the meadow and, even though she wasn't near enough to hear, she imagined the rushing sound of spring water as it fell over the mossy rocks into Thatcher's Pond.

As always this view lightened her spirits. She loved every inch of Wintersfield, all five hundred acres of prime farmland. One day, every tree and rock on the hillside, every one of the furled green shoots that sprouted up in the plowed clearing would belong solely to her. Last night at supper Gus had told her that at the rate she was going, it would only be a few more years before that dream became a reality.

Of course, there had been times since Gordon's death that she'd doubted her ability to purchase Gus Winters's farm. But it was beginning to look as if things were starting to go her way. So far this year, the fates had been kind. The weather had been nothing short of sensational all spring, the dairy stock was in perfect health and the price of milk had reached a new high. Why, even old beat-up Rosie had wheezed herself back and forth from the fields without breaking down a single time. By all indications, it was going to be a very good year, and by anyone's standards, except maybe her mother's, Melissa was successful.

According to Elaine Kvam, Melissa couldn't possibly continue managing the farm by herself. "You need a husband, Melissa, and Kenny needs a father." That was the continuing litany Melissa had been hearing from her mother for the past few months. Elaine had listed every available bachelor in a tri-county area as possibilities, and Melissa wondered how the woman knew them all. But maybe that was a special gift that matchmakers like her mother were born with—this uncanny ability to ferret out the identity, whereabouts and qualifications of every unmarried person within a reasonable range. After that, it became the matchmaker's sole objective to relieve the "miserably single" of their state.

"I'm doing just fine, mom," was Melissa's calm response whenever the subject came up, which was nearly every time she saw her mother. The Kvam farm was in the same county, and Melissa saw her parents at least once a week. For the most part, she was glad they lived so close but more than once of late, when the matchmaking had reached new heights of intensity, Melissa wondered if she should consider relocating.

A sheep ranch in Australia might be good, she mused with a giggle. However, surveying the field in front of her she knew that this was where she wanted to be and this was the farm she wanted to call her own. More than anything she wished to prove that what many called her silly newfangled ideas actually worked and that running a successful farm was not so much a matter of muscle as of brains. *I can do it—and without a husband!*

Her efforts over the past year had gone a long way toward winning her the respect of her neighbors. At church the previous Sunday, Joel Holley, owner of one of the community's largest and most profitable farms, had stepped over and asked her advice. After the last test of her dairy herd, it was found that she'd managed to increase both butterfat and volume.

Word of her accomplishments had spread, and Joel had wanted to learn her secret. She had been happy to tell him about the new mix of feed she was using and the beneficial effects soothing music had on her stock. She had savored the admiring look in Joel's eyes and his compliment for days. "I like your thinking, Mel. I do believe you're really going to make a go of the place."

"Not if you don't start work," Melissa scolded herself aloud, then glanced nervously over her shoulder as the sound of her own voice rose over the roar of the tractor's engine. She shrugged. It wasn't as if there was a soul around to hear her, but she was aware of forming a bad habit that might embarrass her someday in public.

Frowning as much at herself as the field waiting to be sprayed, she tried to recall how long it had been since she'd gone anywhere other than to church or the grocery store and could not. "I really have to do something about this," she told herself briskly. "It's bad enough conversing with a tractor, but now I'm starting to talk to myself. Gus is right. I'd better take some time off and look up a few of my old friends. Rosie's awfully nice but she just doesn't hold up her end of the conversation."

She glanced back over her shoulder to make sure the sprayer was still securely hitched to the tractor, then looked ahead to check between the rows of knee-high corn. She was right. Because of the unusually warm, wet weather they'd enjoyed all spring it was past time to apply the herbicide. Pigweed, foxtail and Johnson grass were already rearing their sinister heads through the black clods of upturned soil. Although spraying for weeds was a filthy job and her least favorite chore, she knew what would happen if she delayed much longer. The invasive weeds would choke the life out of her precious crop of new corn.

With a resolute sigh, she extracted a white gauzy mask from the breast pocket of her blue chambray shirt and adjusted it over her mouth and nose. Next came the thick goggles that would keep the noxious spray out of her blue eyes, then the broad-billed cap to protect her blond hair and finally the wide red bandanna that covered her throat. As she checked for any signs of exposed skin in the side mirror, she had to laugh. She looked like some goo-goo eyed, white-snouted creature from an unknown planet.

Two hours later, she had completed half of the field and was beginning a new round, heading the tractor back into the fine white mist of herbicide that floated in the warm June breeze. Spraying was a repetitive task, and all Melissa really had to do to occupy her time was to hold the tractor steady to avoid injuring the nearby plants. Melissa, an expert driver, could almost do that by feel, her gloved hands automatically making the minor adjustments on the steering wheel as the front wheels flattened the moist soil between rows.

Most of the time, her eyes were free to scan the gravel road that ran parallel to the cornfield, her mind free to play the mental game she had devised to pass the hours. Few cars ever passed by that weren't driven by one of her neighbors. Her challenge was to identify a car and its driver before it crossed the imaginary line she had drawn between two distant telephone poles. If she could do it, she rewarded herself with a swig of soda between rounds; if she could not, she had to wait one extra pass before cooling her thirst.

"That's Mrs. Lathrop in her son's souped-up Ford," she decreed smugly, a quarter mile before the slow-moving car passed between the two poles. "Pull up to the bar, Rosie," she instructed, bringing the tractor to a halt beneath the cooling shade of a tall elm. "This drink is on me."

Lifting her mask, she took a long swallow from the aluminum can she'd tucked into a small Styrofoam cooler. So what if it was a silly game? It alleviated boredom and that was all that was necessary. The caffeine-laced cola might also help her stay awake.

Melissa was acutely aware of what could happen to a farmer who didn't stay constantly on her guard, the danger of forgetting how many powerful horses were housed inside the tractor's benign-sounding engine. No matter how sleepy she became, she couldn't afford to doze, not for a second.

Just such a lapse had cost her a husband and her five-year-old son, Kenny, a father. It had been a senseless accident and never would have occurred if Gordy hadn't been trying to prove he could work a full day after working half the night before. He'd fallen asleep on the job, hadn't been aware of the ominous sound coming from his overworked engine. Melissa would never forget that sound nor the terror she had experienced as she'd raced across the fields shouting her husband's name. He hadn't heard her, and she would carry those last images of him with her to the grave. Even now, more than a year later, she could recall in perfect detail the lazy half smile that had been on his face, the way his closed eyes had shot open a second before he'd been unseated by the bucking tractor.

She would always live with the final, halting words he'd spoken to her as she'd cradled his bleeding head in her lap, the self-derision in his agonized voice. "You were right, Mel. Such a... fool. I've... lost our dream for... good this time. Not much of a man... to let you... down this way."

Letting her down. That had been Gordy's view of every setback they had endured since the day they had gotten married. When they couldn't raise the money to buy a farm outright and had worked out an arrangement with Gus Winters for the future purchase of Wintersfield, that was somehow letting her down. When a cow died and they had lost the profit from its future milk or a hailstorm destroyed a crop, Gordy had always blamed himself. Even Gus, who had lived on a farm for all his sixty-seven years, couldn't convince Gordy that no one was to blame for what nature decreed.

Melissa had always accepted that farming was taking a gamble with nature but, unlike her husband, she thrived on every challenge. When times were hard, she gritted her teeth and worked harder. Though she was strong, and usually optimistic about the future, there had been many times when her resolve had wavered and she would have liked to have turned to Gordy for support. But not wanting to let him down, she had forced herself to stay in control, not realizing her husband had felt she was competing with him and winning. Before they'd married, Gordon had seemed to admire her strengths. Afterward, however, those same qualities had somehow threatened his masculinity.

In the months preceeding his death, he'd even begun to challenge her femininity, telling her, "Sometimes, Mel, you're a better man than I." The passion had died out in their marriage, and Melissa hadn't been able to bring it back. It still hurt when she let herself recall those humiliating times when she had tried without success.

Melissa was convinced she'd never remarry, and didn't want the responsibility of nurturing a man's ego at the risk of her own. Besides misjudging Gordon on other things, she'd been wrong to think that since he was well over six feet tall with a strapping build, he wouldn't be put off by her size. At five feet nine inches tall, big-boned and healthy, she could run the farm machinery, lay in crops and care for the stock as well as or better than any man, including her husband. Too late, she'd discovered that the more she did for the success of the farm, the less Gordy thought of her as a woman.

To Melissa, the most tragic aspect of it all was the view Gordy had taken of his own death. He'd tormented himself to the very end, and Melissa hoped with all her heart that he now enjoyed a full measure of peace. She had to believe that, or she'd find none for herself.

Glancing up at the clear blue sky, Melissa noted by the position of the sun that it was almost noon. She had promised herself that she'd be done spraying by then. Instead, she'd been wasting valuable time with sad thoughts, dwelling on a past that couldn't be changed. Out in the field lay her future, and she was determined to make it a good one. "Let's go, Rosie. Gus and Kenny will be home soon, and this nasty job is going to be done." She pulled up her mask, then rammed the stick shift back into gear.

Nearing the end of her last round, she saw a cloud of dust swirling up along the road. That was an interesting thing in itself, for the size of the cloud meant speed, and hardly anyone drove faster than twenty miles an hour down the winding, graveled road. She judged the distance she had in which to make her identification. Not long.

The car slowed down to take a curve and the dust cleared. Who did she know who drove a dark-blue...Corvette? None of their frugal neighbors had any use for such an impractical vehicle! She could tell that the driver was a man, but that was about all as the low-slung car sped past. "I'm done anyway, so I can still have a drink," she mumbled peevishly, curiosity keeping her eyes narrowed on the shiny Corvette as it slowed down near the driveway of Wintersfield.

He can't be coming here, she thought. Yet it looked as if she was wrong, for in what appeared to be an intentional maneuver, the car turned into the drive and bypassed the one-story rambler Gus had built for himself after the death of his parents. Moments later the car came to a halt near the back porch of the much larger, original farmhouse that Melissa now called home.

She headed for the dirt track that would take her back to the machine shed. When whoever it was didn't get an answer at the house, he'd surely search the barn and the yard and she should be able to cut him off. "It has to be another salesman," she judged with an annoyed sigh, then pressed a little harder on the fuel pedal as she maneuvered the tractor out of the field. On a sunny day like this, she didn't want to waste much time listening to some long-winded sales pitch.

By the time she reached the farmyard, the driver of the Corvette was striding down the drive toward the barn. At the sound of the approaching tractor, he stopped walking and waited for its arrival. Melissa had ample time to size up his appearance as she guided Rosie over the remaining yards of muddy track.

He was definitely not the usual kind of salesman who visited the farm. For one thing, he was much better dressed. For another, he'd arrived in a sports car. Dealers in farm products usually drove up in pickup trucks and wore overalls or at least something washable. The choice of practical attire not only inspired the farmers' trust but was a necessity, as salesmen often met with their prospective customers in barns or fields, sometimes lending a helping hand as they discussed seed, fertilizer or any of the other sundry products essential to farming.

Somehow Melissa didn't think the urbane-looking man in the immaculate white linen slacks, crisp lemon-yellow shirt and expensive-looking tie had come out to sell her the latest brand of insecticide, and she doubted that his flashy Corvette contained sample bags of herbicide or stacks of literature on artificial insemination. Life insurance, she decided, sensing the latent energy behind his unmoving stance. She didn't know why, but men who sold life insurance always looked as if death wouldn't dare touch them. *He's going to try to sell me on triple indemnity,* she decided, even though there was no salesman's welcome on the man's face, only a vague expression of impatience.

Melissa made a thorough study of him through the foggy lenses of her goggles. He stood with feet slightly apart, one hand resting on his hip. When she made no attempt to speed up, his other hand began tugging restlessly at the knot of his tie. She guessed his age to be about thirty-five—an age when most men began showing a bit of paunch. But there wasn't an ounce of spare flesh on him. A curious stabbing sensation began in her stomach, a discomfiting jolt of physical awareness that took her completely by surprise. Not even Gordy, in the impassioned days of their courtship, had inspired such a purely primitive response in her.

There was something about this man that called out to the woman in her, something in his closed expression that sparked her curiosity. He wasn't the most handsome man she'd ever seen but his looks were compelling. His face had hard edges—it was faceted like a rough-cut diamond. There was a worldly cynicism about him, a knowing air that set him apart from any man she knew. For a salesman, he certainly had a commanding air, looking as if he expected to get something from her instead of the other way around.

His brown hair caught the sun, highlighting streaks of gold, and she caught her breath. He had gorgeous hair. Layered away from his face, it was cut short at the ears, a thick unruly lock falling over his tanned forehead to form a high vee at the side part. There was a small square of white gauze taped at his temple, standing out against his bronzed skin. His deep tan made it clear that he was not from this part of the country, for in early June, only the most loyal sun worshipers in Minnesota could boast such a dark color.

Without being aware of it, Melissa slowed down until the tractor was barely crawling. For some reason she felt a bit intimidated. The man's intense brown eyes seemed to cut right through her, as hard-looking as the diamond likeness she had ascribed to his face. His nose was long and straight, maybe a bit too large for the rest of his features. It gave his face more strength than it needed and called attention to the only soft-looking thing about him—his lips. They were almost too full and sensual, and they continually drew her gaze. She wished he would smile or do something to break the sharp challenge in his expression.

She placed his height at five-ten or eleven, yet his aggressive stance, wide shoulders and muscular legs made him seem far taller. Unable to stop herself, her eyes fell below his trim waist to the flat belly and the forceful swell of his thighs straining beneath their fragile linen covering. He was all muscle, all man.

Her fingers shook slightly as she came to the end of the track and reached down to shut off the ignition. She had to establish her own position before he realized how he had affected her, before she handed him a weapon she was certain was an important part of his sales pitch. She doubted many women could say no to him and because of it, he could afford that flashy car and those expensive clothes. She was about to ask him to state his business, but he spoke first, shouting at her over the loud, dying wheezes of Rosie's engine.

"Hey, fella. I don't have all day. Where can I find the boss?" His resonant voice matched the pervasive power in his dark-brown eyes.

Although Melissa was somewhat amused that he thought her a male, she took exception to his impatient tone. She'd expected his first line to be full of sweet honey but it was straight vinegar, and his tone effectively doused her sensual reaction to his looks. If he was trying to sell her something, he was off to a very bad start. She pulled off the mask that covered her nose and mouth. "You're talking to him, mister," she informed shortly.

"Come on, kid," he barked his disbelief. "You're not old enough to be placed in charge of anything, and we both know it. I'm here to see the owner. Where is he?"

The man was downright rude! Even if he thought her a teenage boy, she could have been related to the owner, so it wasn't very wise of him to insult her. He must have learned his sales technique from Attila the Hun. Taking advantage of her high seat on the tractor, she glared down at him. "Look, buddy, whatever you're selling, I'm not interested."

"Selling?" A deep furrow developed between his brows. "Who said I was selling anything?"

That was a ploy that wouldn't work either. She'd heard it too many times. For some reason, most salesmen preferred not to admit their intentions until after they'd generated interest in their product. Then as soon as the customer made a positive comment, the salesman would close in for the kill like a man-eating shark. Judging by this man's expensive tastes, he'd enjoyed some success with that method in the past, but Melissa didn't like it, much preferring an honest approach.

With the agility of long practice, she jumped down from the tractor, landing a few feet in front of him. Then Melissa pulled off her cap and removed her goggles, stuffing them both in the back pockets of her overalls. She hoped he could now read what was a clear dismissal in her eyes. "What do you say we stop wasting each other's time? I don't have all day, either. Why don't you give me your best pitch, then I'll give you the reasons why I'm not buying it. I'd say this whole scenario should take about two minutes, and then we can both get on with our business. Okay?"

She could tell that she had surprised him but didn't know if it was because she had turned out to be a woman or because of what she'd said. It wasn't long before she found out.

"You're sure not a kid."

"No, I'm not," she stated the obvious in a bored tone.

"You're a female," he announced, as if telling her something she didn't already know.

"Have been since birth," she agreed glibly. It was a shame that what he had in looks, he apparently lacked in brains. When it appeared as if he wasn't going to do anything but continue his incredulous staring, she lost patience. "We're not that uncommon, you know. I've heard that women make up at least fifty percent of the adult population. Surely you've seen one of us before."

His right brow rose an infinitesimal fraction, his spiky mahogany lashes flickered in astonishment but then he smiled. It was the smile, that slow, lazy smile revealing a row of straight white teeth, that made her heart slam up against her ribs and her lungs cease to function properly.

"I've run across a few but believe me, none of them have been anything like you," he announced through the teasing curve of his lips. "When did fem lib hit this place?" His burnished eyes slid down her full-breasted, long-legged body, then back up to her wide, soft mouth, staying there as he drawled, "Of course, I'm not saying it wasn't a good idea. I know I wouldn't mind having you around. I'll bet you clean up real well."

"How clever of you to see through my disguise," Melissa said, adding an affected twittering giggle for emphasis. Glancing around nervously as if expecting someone to jump out from behind the machine shed, she said in a conspiratorial voice, her expression completely serious, "I'd hate for this to get around, but I'm really Miss Universe."

There. He deserved her flippant retort. She hoped it effectively convinced him that she wasn't so simple that she couldn't recognize a practiced line and heated gaze for exactly what they were. Was she supposed to turn to jelly because a good-looking man was honoring her with a warm blaze of gold from his dark irises?

His mouth spread into an even wider grin then, a deep chuckle rumbled from his chest. "And I'll bet you've got the measurements to prove it, honey." His eyes gleamed wickedly as they probed beneath her clothing as if looking for confirmation.

There was absolutely no way he could see anything interesting beneath the faded shirt and baggy overalls she wore unless he had a libido that worked overtime. Her womanly curves were completely camouflaged, her long blond hair, damp with sweat, was plastered to her scalp, then hung in snaky ropes to her shoulders. Even a movie star would have been unrecognizable with the stark white powder of herbicide coating everything but the skin around her mouth, nose and eyes. Yet Melissa felt stripped, completely vulnerable to the intimate inspection he was giving her.

It didn't matter that he was probably trying to soften her up so she'd buy something from him; it was still unnerving to be inspected so thoroughly. There couldn't be an ounce of sincerity in his gaze or else his standards must not be very high. There was nothing attractive about her gruesome appearance, and she doubted her "essence de herbicide," that could be detected from yards away, was alluring. Scents that were sold in multigallon drums just didn't have the same effect as those marketed by the ounce in small crystal vials.

"I've got things to do, mister." She dropped any semblance of continuing the ridiculous game, dismissal in her curt tone. "Just get on with it so I can get back to work."

"I thought Bob Jackson was the hired hand." The

man bypassed her order as if she'd never spoken, his gaze hopeful as he surveyed the farmyard. "Where is he? I'd like to talk with him."

So that was it! The arrogant jerk preferred discussing his business with a man. As far as she was concerned, that lost him any chance he'd had to sell her anything. She might have understood his reluctance to deal with someone he thought was too young but not this. "Bob Jackson is almost seventy years old and retired. Wherever you got your information, it's out of date." Her voice rose angrily when he looked at her as if she was just as obtuse as she considered him. "Take my advice, mister. Next time you go out on a call, you'd better do all your homework."

"Calm down, honey," he placated, raising both hands toward her, palms up. "We seem to have gotten our signals crossed. All you have to do is tell me where to find Gus Winters, and we'll clear this up. I'm his—"

"My name's not *honey*, and whether you like it or not, I'm the boss here!" She supposed the devastating smile that accompanied his patronizing words usually charmed the pants off most women—but she wasn't most women.

"The hell you are!" he exploded, the placating expression completely gone. "Where's Gus? He's the one I came to see."

Enough was enough! The man had a colossal nerve talking to her that way. Her blue eyes spit with anger, and her gently arched brows straightened to a thin line. Using her most frigid tone, Melissa ordered, "Well, I'm the one who's telling you to get off my land, buddy."

"My name's not buddy, and this isn't your land any more than it's mine," he snarled, frightening her with the fury in his dark eyes. "According to that sign—" he pointed to the carved wooden arches over the driveway "—this is Wintersfield. As far as I know, it's still owned and run by a Winters."

"Then you don't know very much because I've been running this farm for six years." She was not about to let him think she didn't have complete authority. His manner became more offensive with each passing second.

"But you don't own it, do you?" he demanded. His sensual mouth thinned, making her wonder how she could have ever considered it soft.

"And I don't see how that's any of your business!" she snapped dismissively, turning her back on him as she climbed on the tractor. "I repeat," she continued from her safe position on the seat, "you can get right back in that fancy car of yours and drive on."

He placed himself directly before the tractor's front wheels. "Not until you tell me where I can find Gus Winters."

This man was really the limit! He had the tenacity of a bulldog. She pulled her cap out of her back pocket and squashed it down on her head. "If you still think it will help to talk to him, you can find him at the Eat Shop in town," she informed him waspishly.

With an angry gesture of her thumb, she pointed toward the road. "You'll probably find Bob Jackson there too. But it won't do you any good to talk to either of them; they'll only confirm what I just told you. You've lost this sale, mister, and don't ever bother coming back." Deciding that her hostile speech had put an end to the conversation, she turned on Rosie's ignition, but the man didn't move.

"Oh, I'll be back, honey. You still might not like what I'll be selling you then, but you'll buy it," he warned dangerously. "You can count on it."

"When pigs fly!" Melissa shot back. Placing both hands on the wheel, Melissa pushed in the clutch. No one had ever made her more angry, and she hoped he was stubborn enough to stay where he was. She couldn't wait to see his expression when her wheels sprayed mud all over his expensive white pants. She revved up the engine, the only warning she intended to give. Seconds later, she began her turn, smugly satisfied when the front wheels of the tractor barely missed the man's spotless white shoes.

Swearing, he took an involuntary jump backward. Melissa's eyes widened when she saw him clutch at his rib cage, saw the ashen color of his face, then the blue tinge that suddenly circled his white lips. In his attempt to regain his balance, he stumbled into a rut and almost fell, but managed to stay upright by bending forward at the waist. She couldn't tell if that move had been to save himself or if it was an automatic reaction to severe pain.

Immediately she shut off the engine. "I'm sorry! I didn't know you were hurt," she hollered as she scrambled down from the seat. "I never would've hit you." She ran toward him and reached for his arm. "Can I help you? Will you be all right?"

"Forget it." He angrily shrugged off her helping hand, and, throwing back his shoulders, cast her a dark look. "If you're in such a damn hurry, I won't hold you up."

"Look, mister," Melissa pleaded, worried by the breathlessness in his voice, his pallor and the lines of strain around his mouth and eyes. "You made me angry, but I didn't mean to...."

"Didn't you?" he grated, his lips tight. He swiveled on his heel and began walking down the drive to his car. Appalled, Melissa remained where she was, feeling even more guilty when she saw the difficulty he had getting back into the low-slung Corvette.

Keeping one arm protectively crossed over his midriff, he placed the other on the steering wheel for support, then gingerly eased his body down on the bucket seat. He sat there for a long time as if trying to catch his breath, and with every moment that passed, Melissa felt worse. He was hurt, and her foolish action had caused him even more pain.

The small bandage on his forehead had been his only visible injury, but she was now aware that there must have been others. The way he clutched his ribs indicated that they could have been broken or at least badly bruised, and she wondered if he'd been in a recent car accident. Considering the reckless way he'd driven up the road, that wouldn't have surprised her.

She was even more certain of it when he gunned the Corvette's powerful engine, jammed the car into reverse and backed out, coming within a few inches of hitting a tree. In a forward gear, he careered out of the drive in a whirlwind of wet flying gravel and mud. Heading toward town, he took the first curve

in the road at a speed that should have landed him
in the ditch.

"Hothead!" she shouted at the swirling dust
cloud on the road that was all that remained of her
visitor. "You're going to get yourself killed!"

2

"Mom," Kenny shouted through the screen door. "Can I invite someone over to supper?"

"Sure honey, who?" Melissa called back, knowing that her son had spent the entire afternoon with Gus and his elderly cronies. The child adored every one of the men, for they treated him as if he were another "one of the boys." "Is it Bob?"

Kenny pushed his lips to the mesh, ignoring her question. "He said you wouldn't like uninvited company, but Gus said you wouldn't mind at all."

"I'm sure I won't mind," Melissa agreed, unable to leave the gravy she was stirring without risking lumps. "Run across and tell him we'll be sitting down in about ten minutes. Everything's almost ready, so don't take too long. If it is Bob, you tell him he's never uninvited, all right?"

She didn't get an answer. "Kenny?" She shook her head and craned her neck to see out the window over the kitchen sink. She caught a glimpse of her towheaded son dashing back across the lawn to deliver his message. He was a flash of sturdy brown legs and arms, his overlarge Vikings football jersey flapping around his knees. It looked like she wouldn't find out which one of Gus's friends required a home-cooked meal until he arrived to sit down at her table.

Of course, it really didn't matter who it turned out to be. Every one of the older men who occasionally joined them for a meal appreciated her culinary efforts, made her feel like a world-renowned cook. She smiled and kept on with her stirring. Pot roast, boiled potatoes, green beans and a Jell-o salad hardly qualified as a gourmet meal, but she knew from past experience it would be greeted as such.

Wishing she'd been given a little more advance notice, she frowned down at her ragged cutoffs and faded gingham halter. Having spent most of the day in the fields, she'd taken a long, refreshing shower and shampooed her hair to erase the coating of herbicide, sweat and dirt that had covered her from head to toe. To stay cool, she'd dusted her skin with Jean Naté powder and dressed in the skimpy outfit.

Then, wanting to keep her heavy blond hair off her neck, she'd parted it in the middle and caught it up in two casual pigtails. Her nape was cool, but she looked about sixteen instead of twenty-six. If she had known there would be someone besides family for supper, she would have changed into a blouse and skirt, but it was too late for that now. She couldn't leave the stove, and their visitor would just have to take her as she was.

Melissa had far more reason to regret her attire when the screen door burst open and Kenny led Gus and "friend" into the back hall. White slacks, lemon-yellow shirt, white shoes! Her smile of welcome faded the instant she saw that their guest was none other than that bad-tempered, egotistical salesman she had kicked off the farm just hours before! What on earth was he doing here? No wonder he'd told Kenny she wouldn't be pleased if he showed up for supper. She certainly wasn't.

Her half-stunned, half-angry reaction to his presence must have been transparent, for the man's grin was like that of a satisfied cat who had just dined on a particularly tasty canary. His twinkling eyes probed her figure from top to bottom, assessing her vital statistics with the efficiency of a tape measure. To her horror, amusement tugged at his lips at the sight of her scruffy pigtails and increased when he noted her shuffling bare feet.

"Hi," he greeted as if she should have been expecting him all along. His smile changed to the slow, lazy smile he'd first bestowed on her hours ago. However, now it took on a mocking character, as if daring her to bring up the details of their meeting.

"Hello, yourself," she responded indignantly.

"Got some hungry fellas here, Mel," Gus announced. "We would've given you more warning, but we've been tramping all over the farm," he apologized, evidently assuming her less than enthusiastic greeting was due to the short notice he'd given her.

Hoping to placate her further, he went on, "I've already let the cows in the barn so they'll be ready for milking by the time we're done eating." Gus removed his muddy boots, placed them on the papers by the back door, then watched until Kenny had done the same. "You go wash your hands, son, while I introduce Travis to your mom."

Melissa's derisive sniff was almost audible. The man was a very fast worker if he and Gus were already on a first-name basis. Normally Gus didn't talk to strangers that readily. Her brows rose when Gus clasped his hand over his companion's shoulder and ushered him farther into the kitchen. To Melissa's chagrin, they came to a stop right beside her. She took an exaggerated step away.

"Mel, I want you to meet my nephew," Gus began, his weather-worn features creased into a broad smile. "The one I'm always talking about. He came all the way from South America. We're going to have a good, long visit." He left the two of them together while he walked across the room and sat down at the round oak table.

Melissa's head shot up. Nephew! She couldn't have heard Gus correctly.

Not seeing her dismayed expression, Gus continued, "I take it you two didn't get around to exchanging names this afternoon when Travis was here looking for me. We'll take care of that now. Melissa Lindstrand, this is my brother Geoff's son, Travis Winters."

"Nice to see you." Travis's teasing dark eyes trailed down her body, lingering on her peach-toned bare midriff. "Again." He tacked on the last word for Gus's benefit, but she knew he wasn't referring to their renewed acquaintance. What a nerve! What if he was Gus's relative? That didn't give him the right to strip off her clothes with his eyes, and it surely didn't mean she had to like him.

"It was awfully nice of you to invite me to supper," he drawled. A picture of nonchalance, he leaned up against her sink, stretched out his long legs and crossed his ankles in front of him. "Are you sure my showing up here like this hasn't put you out?"

Oh, she was put out all right, but it had nothing to do with having an unexpected guest for supper. "Not at all," she managed, taking a quick step away from him on the pretext of reaching for the salt shaker. A delicate pink mounted in her cheeks as she recalled a few of the more sarcastic comments she'd made to him that afternoon, especially that ridiculous allusion to being Miss Universe. "You're really Geoff's boy?"

Golden shards danced mischievously in his eyes. "Boy? I haven't been a boy for a good many years." He swiveled around to look at his uncle. "What've you been telling this pretty lady, Gus?"

Pretty? No one with half an eye could look at her right now and call her pretty. She wasn't wearing a lick of makeup, her hair hung down in two straggly clumps, and she was practically dressed in rags. Fulsome compliments fell off his tongue as easily as a frog jumping off a log! Unfortunately they still had the desired effect, and Melissa felt her blush spread to her toes. If only she'd put on more clothes, shoes, some kind of armor to protect herself from those incredible eyes that hadn't missed a single detail. At least now his attention was on Gus for a change.

Supremely grateful for the few seconds she'd been given to recover her equilibrium, she turned back to the stove as Gus's booming laughter erupted from his place at the kitchen table. "But you *were* a boy the last time I saw you, Travis," he said. "Guess you never grew up in my mind. Whenever I talk about you, I remember that pesky nine-year-old kid who followed me around like a pup. Remember? That was the year you stayed with us the whole summer. Every time I turned around, you were standing there, bending my ear."

"I remember." It was Travis's turn to flush, and Melissa was surprised at his embarrassment. He didn't look like the type of man who'd ever be self-conscious, especially not by Gus's laughing recollection of what he'd been like as a child. She was even more surprised when he walked away from her. Standing by the table, he changed the subject to something that wouldn't embarrass either one of them instead of attempting to punish her a little more for what had occurred between them that afternoon.

"This smells awfully good, Melissa," Travis said, hungrily eyeing the meat platter in the center of the table. "It's been awhile since I've had a decent meal."

"Why, Mel's the best dang cook in Washington County," Gus decreed, his gray eyes lit with affection as he reached for a hot biscuit. "Her biscuits took a blue ribbon at the state fair last August. Kenny and I were so proud, we nearly busted the buttons on our Sunday shirts."

Gus took a large bite of the warm bread, then sighed with satisfaction. "Light as air. Set yourself down and try one, Travis. You'll find none better."

"A woman of many talents," Travis remarked, but his tone conveyed little warmth.

"Yup, and she's like a daughter to me. Treats me like a king."

To Melissa's dismay, Gus continued listing her talents. "Mel's got a degree in home economics, you know. She taught for a couple of years at the high school but then decided she'd rather be a full-time farmer. That sure didn't set back her cooking any." He patted the ample stomach protruding beneath his bib overalls. "I've put on ten pounds since you started feeding me up, haven't I, Mel?"

"Twenty, but who's counting?" Melissa grinned cheekily, trying valiantly to act normal. She glanced once at Travis and was instantly sorry she had. Those deep-brown eyes of his were focused directly on her again, and it looked as if her examiner was none too pleased with his findings.

Travis was fighting off an unreasonable twinge of jealousy. Still, even knowing he was being childish, he felt resentful. Back when he'd been a boy, Uncle Gus had looked at him like he was viewing Melissa now, but a lot of years had gone by since then. *It's my own fault that I've lost touch,* he reminded himself, but that didn't make it any easier to swallow. He'd foolishly believed he and his uncle could resume their relationship exactly where they'd left off, that nothing would've changed—but now he knew he'd been wrong. Now Melissa and Kenny Lindstrand seemed to occupy the place he'd once had in his uncle's heart.

Feeling Travis's eyes cutting into her, Melissa turned away, ostensibly to reach for a bowl that would hold the gravy. Whatever was displeasing him had something to do with her relationship with Gus. She was used to Gus talking about her as if she was his daughter, but Travis seemed taken aback. He'd done an admirable job of hiding his reaction, but she'd seen the question in his probing eyes. Evidently he and Gus had not spent the afternoon talking about her, or he would've already learned that she was more to Gus than a tenant.

She was glad she hadn't been the major topic of conversation. The less Travis knew about her, the better she'd like it. He already had her at a distinct disadvantage, and she didn't like the position one little bit.

Travis looked down at the table that was only set for three, then back up at the tall flustered blonde who appeared to be glued to the range. She wasn't looking at him, so she didn't notice his indecision. He supposed he should sit down at the empty place and assume she'd provide him with utensils, but he'd prefer to wait until she gave those directions herself. He cleared his throat, but she didn't look up until he gave a rather obvious cough.

"Should I sit here, Melissa, or won't Kenny be joining us for supper?"

She made a flustered gesture with her hands. "I'm sorry. I...I'll set you a place." Her movements were jerky as she reached into the cupboards over the kitchen counter. "Kenny," she called over her shoulder, "supper's ready."

Travis couldn't help feeling satisfied at her show of nerves. After that stunt she'd pulled with the tractor, she was lucky he hadn't made this meeting even more uncomfortable for her than it already was. It had taken him almost twenty minutes to get over the pain. He'd driven out of her sight, then stopped to recover his breath before going on to the restaurant where she'd told him he could find his uncle.

He'd been about to tell Gus about his run-in with the dense, bad-tempered amazon who'd tried to mow him down with her tractor, when he'd been introduced to a five-year-old boy who had turned out to be the amazon's son. When Kenny had acted so pleased to be meeting the nephew Gus always talked about, Travis hadn't had the heart to make any disparaging remarks about the boy's mother. Between the barrage of inquiries thrown at him by Gus and Bob Jackson, he'd learned that Melissa Lindstrand was a widow and the best farmhand Gus had ever had.

Now that he'd seen her and learned more about her, he wondered why she was doing menial labor. She supposedly had a degree in home economics. Why wasn't she putting it to good use? Surely any job in her field would pay better than what she was getting from Gus. Then again, he'd heard the grandiose opinion she had of her position. He wondered if Gus knew that when he was away, his female hired hand told people she was the boss who ran the place.

Despite himself, Travis was intrigued by her. That afternoon when he'd encountered her, she'd looked like an escapee from a spook show. Her throaty voice had been the only thing about her that gave any promise of the woman he might find beneath the disguise.

Discovering that the figure on the tractor wasn't a kid had been the first surprise of the afternoon and not the greatest by a long shot. No, the greatest surprise was walking into her kitchen tonight, and seeing how well "she'd cleaned up," that she really *did* have the measurements to back up her claim of being Miss Universe. He'd expected to find a homely frump, probably with muscles bulging in her arms and legs. Instead, he'd been confronted with long, smooth legs, a tight derriere his hands itched to cup, a small waist and high full breasts.

She was a farmhand, a mother and a seductive siren, all wrapped up into one delightful package. Her sexuality was as natural as the corn-silk color of her hair, the sky-blue depths of her large eyes and the delectable contours of her generous mouth. What made her even sexier was that she seemed completely unaware of her appeal.

He was used to women who made full use of their feminine powers, bartering their bodies in exchange for expensive presents, social position or a meal ticket. Perhaps it was because he instinctively knew Melissa wasn't like that that she presented such a challenge to him. He sensed a dormant sensuality in her just waiting to be awakened.

What was the matter with all the men around here, anyway? There ought to be a line a mile long begging for a glimpse of her. Of course, what did he know? Maybe the voluptuous widow Lindstrand had a dozen men, maybe a special *one*. It was no business of his, except he had this sudden primitive desire to drive them all away—at least while he was staying there.

"Goin' to stand there all night, Travis?" Gus inquired. "Don't be so blasted polite. Mel won't mind if you set yourself down before she comes to the table. We're all family here."

A bit more gingerly than he would have liked,

Travis lowered himself into the chair. The long flight, the drive from the airport plus the severe jolt when he'd jumped out of the tractor's way had all made his middle ache almost as much as when he'd been airlifted out of South America right after the explosion. He tried to cover his wince by smiling at the beaming little boy who slid into the chair next to his, but Gus noticed the tension flit across his face.

"Busted ribs can hurt like the devil," he stated sympathetically. "I got kicked by a cow a few years back, and I thought sure I'd never breathe right again. Got 'em taped up, don't you?"

"Mmm," Travis agreed, trying to downplay his pain. "I'm on the mend. I—"

"What kind of a bomb was it? Must'a been an atom bomb to blow up a bridge that big." As Kenny's excited speech drew everyone's attention a thatch of light-blond hair fell over his forehead, and he impatiently brushed it away. Leaning forward in his chair, his gaze was worshipful. "Did ya' have to shoot anybody? Was it like a real war?"

As Travis began to answer, Melissa tried to assimilate what she'd heard. Bomb? War? She remembered Gus having told her that his nephew was some sort of engineer and that he traveled all over the world, but Gus had never inferred that there was any danger involved in Travis's job. She was as impatient as her son to hear his answer and tried to ignore the twinges of guilt that curled in her stomach.

His injuries weren't the result of his own recklessness but were caused by something beyond his control. She now had further proof that she had misjudged him. He'd been hurt in some kind of explosion, and she'd tried to run him down with a tractor. She felt as if she'd kicked a helpless puppy. Well, he wasn't exactly a helpless puppy. No man who looked at a woman the way he did could be called helpless, but that knowledge didn't dispel her self-condemnation.

"Sorry to disappoint you, Kenny, but I'm not a soldier, just an ordinary engineer trying to do my job." Travis chose his words carefully. He didn't want to romanticize the incident. There was nothing romantic about it or his part in it. He was not the hero in some high adventure but the victim of a senseless attack. "There was no bomb and no war."

"Then how did that bridge blow up and who did it?" Kenny was undaunted in his pursuit. "I heard you tell Gus that pieces of the bridge were flyin' everywhere and some re...revo...."

"Revolutionaries," Travis supplied. "In some countries, like the one where I was in South America, Kenny, there are men who dislike their governments so much that they'd do anything to cause trouble."

"Didn't they want a new bridge?"

"Yes, but they didn't like a foreign company building it."

"Then how come they didn't build it themselves?" Kenny asked, his face screwed up in a quizzical frown.

Patiently Travis went on, "In the country where I was working, they didn't have the equipment or know-how to build the kind of bridge they needed. The company I work for builds things all over the world. We try to help people who can't do the job themselves. Usually they're happy to have us, but this time we ran into some men who wanted to scare us away."

"But they didn't scare you, did they?" Kenny persisted.

Travis was taken aback. He hadn't had many dealings with children before and certainly not one who was determined to make him out as a hero. It was inflating to the ego, and for a moment he was tempted to let the child believe what he wanted, but he knew that would be unfair. Hadn't he grown up listening to glorified war stories only to discover later that there was nothing to admire in the man who told them?

"They did scare me, Kenny," Travis confessed matter-of-factly. "Any man is scared when he thinks he's about to die."

"Travis is right, Kenny," Gus interposed. "Only a fool wouldn't be scared, but a brave man does what needs to be done even if he's shaking in his boots. I'll bet even though Travis got hurt himself, he made sure his crew was safe before seeing to his injuries."

Travis glowered at the older man and negated the praise with a slow shake of his head. "This brave man was knocked unconscious by the explosion, and by the time I came to I was on my way to a hospital. All I did was supply a list of names to the rescuers, hardly reason for a medal."

Melissa was impressed with Travis's explanation. He didn't talk down to Kenny, nor did he exaggerate. Some men would have taken advantage of the obvious hero-worship in Kenny's eyes, but Travis did not. He seemed reluctant to say much more about the incident and deftly changed the subject. "Tell me about those cat families I saw out in the barn, Kenny," Travis asked.

In the few seconds before her son began listing his numerous pets and their various personalities, Melissa saw a haunted look in Travis's eyes. She sensed that the hurt he'd received in that explosion had not been just physical.

She approached the table with his place setting, her impressions of Travis modified once again. He might be brash, arrogant in his ability to rattle her composure but she wondered if there weren't a few cracks in his confident facade. Cracks or no cracks, he had a disturbing effect on her.

While Travis continued querying Kenny about his interests, his rich timbered voice set chills down the center of Melissa's back. She almost jumped when she felt his linen-covered thigh press against her bare leg. She knew the move had been deliberate when he advised, "It's hard for me to reach for things. Can you put my water glass a little closer to my plate?" His expression was innocent, but his eyes sparkled with challenge.

In order to fulfill his request, she'd have to take a step closer and reach across him. "Certainly," she replied with forced politeness. His thigh was there waiting for the touch of her leg when she moved, his eyes gleaming with appreciation as she bent over the table and her full, rounded breasts swung into view. Her fingers shook as she set the glass in front of him and immediately straightened up.

"Thanks for being so accommodating," Travis

said innocently. When she heard him swallow hard, a fiery blush heated her entire body.

She felt confused—both ashamed and excited. His smile was benign, but she saw the invitation in his eyes. She was allowing a man she hardly knew to get past her defenses, and it made her furious. He had the uncanny ability to make her feel small and feminine, like an extremely desirable woman, and she knew she was not. She turned her back to him, struggling for control as she hurried to the counter for the rest of their meal.

As she picked up a bowl of vegetables and another of potatoes, she bit her lip, silently cursing the creator of halter tops, especially the kind that gaped beneath the arms and did such an insufficient job of concealing her suddenly taut nipples. She'd made this stupid thing herself to use as a sample for her beginning sewing class. Oh, the sewing assignment had been easy all right—just a rectangular scrap of fabric gathered between two strings. Why hadn't she had them make aprons like every other beginning class.

Aprons. Now there was a good idea. Where was her all-encompassing cobbler apron? She had almost decided to go find it when she realized how strange it would look to put on an apron *after* cooking the meal. There was no help for it, she'd have to brazen it out. Squaring her shoulders, she returned to the table, plunked down the food, then yanked out her chair and sat down.

"Are you sure my being here doesn't bother you?" Travis asked, not quite able to hide his quicksilver grin.

"Of course it doesn't," she lied.

"What did I tell you, Travis?" Gus beamed his approval. "I'm always bringing somebody home for dinner, and Mel never blinks an eye. She keeps telling me there's nothing to putting on an extra plate, and she always cooks enough for an army."

"And it's going to get cold if we don't start eating," Melissa stated calmly, then turned to her son and instructed, "Kenny, will you please say grace?"

When the prayer was completed, Melissa picked up the bowl of potatoes and passed it to their guest, trying not to cringe as his warm, blunt-tipped fingers came into contact with hers. She let go of the bowl as soon as she could and prepared to hand him another. The quicker this meal got under way, the quicker it would be over.

When the food had all been passed and everyone's plate was full, Melissa began eating like there was no tomorrow. Shoveling her portion down at a pace that was destined to cause an acute case of indigestion, she didn't notice that no one else was eating until she felt their astounded eyes on her. It took three tries before she was able to swallow what she'd crammed into her mouth. "Is something the matter?" she mumbled, reaching for her water glass.

"Gee, mom. You sure must be hungry." Kenny's blue eyes were as wide as she'd ever seen them. "You forgot—"

"I didn't forget anything," she interrupted with annoyance. "Everything I cooked is on the table. Now let's hurry up, so we won't be late with the milking." Noticing her son's untouched plate, she admonished sharply, "You know you're not to dawdle over your food, Kenny. Why haven't you started eating?''

Gus's bushy gray brows rose as he came to Kenny's defense. ''We're dawdling because we don't have enough silverware to go around. Which one of us is supposed to share with Travis?''

Startled, Melissa turned and noticed Travis's lack of silverware. ''Well, why didn't you say something?'' she reproached.

Scraping her chair back so abruptly that she had to grab it to keep it from falling to the floor, she stormed across the kitchen. As she yanked open the silverware drawer, she muttered under her breath. ''Helpless. All males are helpless! For God's sakes, why couldn't one of them have done this themselves?''

As she fiddled with the flatware in the drawer to find a matching set, she heard Gus's soft-spoken comment, ''I don't know what's gotten into her. She's not usually like this.''

Worse, she heard Travis's rejoinder, as she was sure she was meant to. ''She could've had a rough day. Maybe something came up that she didn't know how to handle.''

''My mom can handle anything.'' Loyally Kenny disagreed, not bothering to lower his voice. ''She didn't even lose her temper when old Bossy stepped on her foot.''

''Have your toes been stepped on lately, Melissa?'' Travis inquired silkily.

Well aware of his double meaning, Melissa groped for an equally barbed response, but her mind went blank. Not liking the feeling, she wondered how long Travis planned on staying, hoping the visit was merely a brief stopover on his way to someplace else, someplace very far away. He was much too adept at getting under her skin. She didn't want to be uncivil to him in front of his uncle—who obviously thought the world of him—but he was really asking for it. The guilt she'd felt over the tractor incident was being replaced by irritation.

As she returned to the table to give him his silverware, a saccharine smile was plastered on her face. "I'm usually pretty fast on my feet. How 'bout yourself?"

"Oh, I generally manage to jump clear of most things," Travis retorted easily. "Course, I've had some close calls lately, but nothing I can't handle."

To Melissa's relief, Gus didn't pick up on the hidden meaning of their exchange. "Well whatever riled you today, you just forget it and enjoy this fine meal you fixed. Don't you worry 'bout the milkin', either. We men'll take care of it tonight." He nudged Kenny's shoulder. "Right son? Your mom's worked hard sprayin' all day and deserves a night off. She can keep Travis company while we do the evenin' chores."

Travis looked pleased at that prospect, but Melissa was not. "I'm not that tired, Gus," she protested.

"Nonsense." Gus held up his hand. "You're all cleaned up and smelling pretty, and I'm still in my working clothes. Let me do this for you, Mel. My arthritis has been acting up all day cuz I didn't do anything but sit. Moving around keeps me from stiffening up."

When Kenny jumped on Gus's suggestion with obvious approval, she knew she'd lost the battle.

Both of them thought they were doing her a favor, and she couldn't tell them she didn't want it. "Thanks," she murmured. "I'll have a treat waiting for you when you get back in. How about some homemade ice cream?"

"Your ice cream's the best." Kenny's eyes lit up. "Can we have chocolate?"

"Is that all right with you, Gus?" Melissa asked.

"You know me. I'll eat anything. Why don't you ask Travis what flavor he likes."

Travis glanced at Melissa, his eyes flicking over her lips, then away. "I had this sudden urge for strawberry, but you asked first, Kenny." He smiled at the boy before turning back to Melissa. "Since I'm going to be here for a while, I'll see if I can't convince your mom to indulge me with that flavor some other time."

3

MELISSA TOOK OUT HER FRUSTRATION on a cloth bag of ice, swinging it repeatedly against the stone walkway in front of the house. When she dumped the contents of the canvas sack into the outer bucket of the ice-cream maker, she was abashed by the results of her virulent feelings. She'd been so carried away by the picture she'd formed of Travis's face on the flagstone that she'd gone far beyond crushing the ice. she'd practically decimated the large cubes into powdered snow.

As she began alternating layers of rock salt with the "snow," she grumbled, "We'll be lucky if this even turns the cream into slush." She glanced over her shoulder at the house, glaring through the screen door. If the ice cream was ruined, it would be all Travis Winters's fault. His insolent remarks about strawberries had destroyed her good intentions to be polite to him. The accompanying look on his face had established an intimacy between them he'd had no right to assume. "It'll be a cold day in hell before I indulge that man in anything," she vowed.

As she poured a rich mixture of eggs, cream, sugar and chocolate into the inner cylinder, her humor didn't improve, and she couldn't prevent an unlady-

like curse when she slopped some of the thick concoction on her arm. "Blast the man!"

"Shouldn't let a single drop of that go to waste,"
Travis's deep voice rumbled close behind her.

"I thought you were still in the kitchen," she accused, wondering with no small amount of unease if
he had overheard her last comment. That unease
rose to astronomical heights when Travis's large,
broad hand grasped her wrist and guided her fore-
arm to his lips.

"Mmm, that's good," he complimented as he
licked the splotch of sweet, chocolate-flavored cream
off her soft skin.

She jerked her arm away from him and immediately thrust it under the yard spigot, rinsing away
the sticky residue along with the memory of the feel
of his tongue. "Surprised you think so since it's not
your favorite flavor," she snapped sarcastically, and
wiped her arm dry on the seat of her cutoffs. Intent
on ignoring him, she slammed the dasher into the
ice-cream maker. Then, with a flourish, she attached
the lid and handle.

Melissa knelt down on the grass, keeping her eyes
firmly fixed on her task. She was determined not to
let Travis know that his touch had done far more
than make her angry. Unfortunately, having him
standing so close behind her kneeling figure was
just as disconcerting as his touch. Every nerve in her
body was aware of him, every muscle finely tuned to
his presence. If she swiveled around, her eyes would
encounter....

"I'm going up on the porch to crank this," she got
out breathlessly. "The mosquitoes are starting to

bite." She grabbed up the heavy wooden tub and stalked off.

"Melissa," Travis called softly, and she halted just before the steps but kept her back to him. "I'm sorry I make you so angry."

She whirled around to face him, clutching the cold burden in her arms as if it was a protective shield. "Then why do you keep doing it? You've done nothing but tease and torment me since you stepped foot on this property."

"I hardly think it's been one-sided," he riposted with a maddening grin. Before she could counter his accusation he elaborated, "Maybe I do it because you're so gorgeous when you blush, or because I like the way your incredible blue eyes flash fire when you try so hard to hold on to your temper."

That was it! She'd really had it with his meaningless praise. She had no false modesty about her looks. She was a big, strapping farm girl. Wholesome was the most truthful compliment she could expect from a man. She shifted the ice-cream maker to one hip. "Look, you can stop with the compliments. There's nobody here to impress with your gallantry! I am not gorgeous when I blush or any other time, and there is nothing outstanding about my eyes. I don't know how long you spent in South America, but it must have been long enough to forget how common blue eyes are in Minnesota. Mine aren't any different than anybody else's!"

"My God, you really believe that, don't you?" he asked, his incredulity evident in his voice.

"Of course I do. I see myself in a mirror every day. There's absolutely nothing—"

"Oh, yes there is," he interrupted as he closed the space between them. "South America has its fair share of sexy women and some of them are blue-eyed blondes. Believe it, Melissa...." His voice lowered to a raspy whisper, and his eyes held hers in a powerful snare. "Your eyes *are* incredible and so is the rest of you."

She remained immobile, staring at him until he lifted both hands toward her face. She took a step backward, her expression stormy. "Don't," she ordered, shakily.

"*You* don't."

His softly delivered command was infinitely more effective than if he'd bellowed at her. She felt his fingers gently sliding the cloth-covered bands from her hair, then winnowing through the unconfined strands before he let the glimmering silver-gold length spill over her shoulders.

"It's a little cooler now, and this is much too pretty to keep tied up." He gave her an imploring look. "Please, don't try to tell me your hair's not pretty or that it's not unusual. Trust me, it is."

"I...I...ah...better get started cranking." Melissa began backing away, moving sideways up the stone steps until she came up against the screen door. She pushed it open with her backside. He followed her every inch of the way.

From the step below, Travis was going to reach around her to hold the door open but had to forego the polite gesture when the stretching action strained the muscles across his injured ribs. "Damn," he muttered. "I can't even open a door for a lady."

Melissa made her way through the door as planned

and stood against it to keep it open until Travis stepped safely inside the porch. Her voice softened with genuine concern as she asked, "You were hurt pretty badly, weren't you?"

"Bad enough."

His terse answer spoke volumes. She remembered the haunted look in his eyes when he'd been speaking with Kenny at supper, and again she wondered what other wounds he'd sustained besides the visible injuries. The probability seemed high that someone he cared about could have been killed in that explosion.

Even knowing he might consider it prying, curiosity prompted her to ask, "Did you lose a good friend in the explosion?"

"There were casualties, yes," he evaded, and turned his face away to survey the porch. There was a clear dismissal in the tense outline of his shoulders. "I'm glad to see that some things haven't changed around here. I remember that old porch swing and the rockers. My grandparents sat out here every night during the summer. They used to point out the constellations to me."

Melissa took the hint and remarked, "Gus does that with Kenny now."

Noting the short-lived but resentful look on his face, she didn't elaborate further. She supposed it had come as quite a shock to him to find someone else living in the Winterses' ancestral home. Still, Gus had insisted that she and Gordy move in, saying he just didn't need all that space and could no longer manage the upkeep. There was no reason for her to feel guilty, even if Travis's reminiscence had sounded so wistful.

Her thoughts took an entirely different turn when Travis sauntered into the circular beam cast by the overhead porch light. His gold-streaked brown hair was bathed in the glow. Melissa felt the tiny hairs at her nape rise with sudden tension and was immediately conscious of how long it had been since she'd shared this porch with a man who wasn't twice her age.

There was nothing even remotely elderly about Travis as he hitched up his pant legs, then lowered his muscled frame onto the wooden porch swing. Although she was fighting off an acute attack of nerves, he seemed perfectly relaxed. He brought one ankle across his knee, then began pushing the swing into slow motion with his foot.

Why did he have to sit like that? Didn't he realize that his flexed leg allowed a prominent display of the back of his thigh, the conspicuous swelling at one side of his inseam? Melissa's eyes darted to his fingers that were clasped around his ankle, lingered on the golden sheen of hair sprinkled over the back of his hand. An unbidden picture came into her mind, a picture of that hand roaming over her body, those long fingers exploring her.

"Are you going to put that thing down somewhere or just hold it?" he asked with a devilish grin. "If you keep hugging it like that, we'll end up with hot chocolate instead of ice cream."

For a moment Melissa simply stared at him, then felt her face burning. She could have kicked herself for letting him know that he bothered her. Trying to overcome the feeling that she'd just made a total fool out of herself, Melissa set the ice-cream maker down on a stool, then promptly positioned herself on the wicker rocker behind it, placing her legs on either side of the outer bucket.

Slowly she started turning the crank. Only the sloshing sound of the cream being swirled by the rotating dasher and the occasional creak of the swing's chain grating against the metal hooks in the ceiling broke the summer silence.

Travis wished Melissa had chosen to sit someplace else. How could she spread her legs apart like that and not know what it did to him? Didn't she realize what view she was affording him of the soft flesh of her inner thighs? With every forward motion of the metal crank, he was rewarded with the tantalizing jiggle of full breasts, the rise and fall of one luscious curve. His fingers tingled with the urge to hold the weight of her in his hands, and he jammed them into the front pockets of his pants. The grating of the swing took on a faster tempo.

Unable to stand the unbearable tension stretched between them, Melissa blurted, "Why are you staring like that? Haven't you ever seen someone make ice cream before?"

"My grandmother used to make gallons of it, sitting in the same chair as you are now. Somehow, she didn't lend such flair to the process."

She shot him a skeptical glance. "I hope you're not planning to tell me that along with my incredible eyes and hair, you think there's something special about the way I make ice cream?"

Melissa's breath strangled in her throat when his flaring golden-brown eyes became riveted on the agitated movements of her breasts. Unable to handle such a flagrant perusal, she looked away, staring at the warped planks under her bare feet.

He gave a low, husky chuckle. She was delightfully naive, and his visit took on an unexpectedly pleasant dimension. Knowing he was taking unfair advantage, he still couldn't resist finding out how far he could push her before she put him in his place. "It's not how you make ice cream that intrigues me."

She missed his triumphant grin as she walked right into his trap. "Oh really, then what does?"

With a tone as smooth as silk, he drawled, "I was sitting here wondering which would taste better, the ice cream or the incredible breasts of the woman making it."

"Oh!" Melissa gasped, dumbfounded. No man had ever said anything that suggestive to her before. She looked around to make sure that neither Gus nor Kenny had come back to the house. "Look, you...you...I don't know what kind of woman you think I am, but around here people don't talk like that! If Gus had heard you say something like that, you'd be run off the farm."

His grin didn't fade. "If you gave me a sample of what I want, that might be worth it."

"I don't give free samples," she retorted hotly, completely unprepared for his immediate comeback.

"Really? Well then, how much do you charge?"

Melissa's garbled sputter made Travis laugh, but then he took pity on her. "I'm sorry, Melissa, but you're such an easy target. I couldn't help myself. If you promise not to run off in a huff, I'll behave myself."

"If you behave yourself, I won't dump this ice cream over your head," Melissa shot back.

"That's a deal."

Travis leaned back against the swing, perfectly content to go on watching the fascinating woman before him. He'd discovered a lot from that conversation. She'd need a little courting before giving in to him. Courting. Now there was an old-fashioned term that suited Melissa perfectly.

The silence between them went on and on and on. Melissa had to say something, even if it meant provoking another round of teasing. Choosing what she hoped was a safe subject, she asked, "Travis, why have you come?"

"To visit Uncle Gus. Why else?"

"But you haven't visited your uncle once in the six years I've been here. Why now?"

He stopped rocking the swing. Melissa tensed in anticipation. She was prying again but couldn't seem to help herself. Maybe this time, he'd just come right out and tell her to mind her own business.

"I'm not really sure," he finally began, pushing the swing into easy motion again. "I suppose I needed to be with family."

"I can understand that." His closed expression made her nervous, and she found herself asking a barrage of questions. "I would imagine your parents were worried sick about you. Have you been to see them? Let them know you're still in one piece? I heard your dad is stationed in Washington. Did you stop off there before coming here?"

"No," he stated tersely, then as if realizing it wouldn't be polite to let it go at that went on, "I've been out of touch with my parents for quite some time now and saw no reason to concern them with this. I'll be fine."

She was subjected to an intense scrutiny. "You seem to know a lot about my family."

His tone was brittle, and she noticed a betraying pulse in his jaw. She wished she'd never mentioned his parents. "Not really. All I know is that Gus is very proud of his brother."

"That surprises me," Travis admitted. "I always thought dad's staying in the army after World War Two was a disappointment to the rest of the family."

"I wouldn't know about that," she confessed uncomfortably. "Gus has always described your father in the most glowing terms. He likes to brag a little to his cronies at the Eat Shop about his brother, the Pentagon general."

Travis's laugh was short. "Yeah, my old man has an impressive title all right."

Melissa shot him a questioning glance. What was she supposed to say to that? Sensing she wasn't going to get more information from him, she cleared her throat and said, "I met your parents once. They seemed very nice."

"Really? When?" Travis inquired with seeming disinterest, but his curiosity was pricked.

"It was...." Her voice trailed off for a moment, then came back. "They stopped in for a few days on their way to Washington. It was not long after Gordy was killed. I don't really remember much except that they were very kind to me, especially your mother."

"Yeah, Priscilla's good at consoling widows. It's part of her job," Travis said dryly.

Again, Melissa was startled, both by the bitterness she sensed behind the words and his disdainful use of his mother's given name. She would have questioned him further, but Travis stopped the inquiry she was about to make with an impatient wave of his hand. He shook his head. "Forget I said that, I didn't mean to bring up the death of your husband."

"It's all right. It's been over a year now."

Travis didn't know why but he was compelled to ask, "Do you still miss him?"

Melissa didn't answer right away. Of course she missed Gordy, even if it wasn't in the way most people assumed. She missed him because he'd been so much a part of her life for so many years, and had been the father of her son. She had grieved for Gordy, not because he was gone for her but because he'd been too young to die and his death had been so unnecessary. It shouldn't have happened and wouldn't have if Gordy hadn't been so dispirited, so insecure. "Yes, Gordy was a good man," she finally said.

Travis felt a painful stab the moment she answered. It astonished him. Why should her grief, her hurt affect him like this? Why did it bother him that she still missed her husband? He was as intrigued by his reaction as he was by the woman herself. He didn't understand it, but he had the strongest sensation that she represented the part of his life that had always been missing. How could that be possible? He'd just met her.

The sun was beginning to go down, the dark

shadows of the tall oaks just beyond the porch
stretched across the smooth planks veiling Melissa's
features with the dusky light. Travis glanced over
his shoulder toward the barn, wondering how much
more time he might have alone with her before Gus
and Kenny returned from the barn. The lights were
still on inside the milk house, and he assumed Gus
was in the final stage of the milking process.

When he and Gus had arrived at Wintersfield that
afternoon, Gus had taken Travis on a quick tour of
the farm, proudly pointing out the changes and improvements that had been made. The long dairy
barn was much the same, but the milk house was
new, and Gus had enthused at length on "Mel's"
newfangled ideas. She had designed the concrete-
block building, the arrangement of tanks and sinks,
implemented more efficient methods of getting the
job done quickly and hygienically. According to
Gus, since "Mel" had started working on the farm,
Wintersfield's milk production had increased in
amount as well as grade.

Now that Travis reflected upon Gus's discussion,
he realized how little had been said about Gordon
Lindstrand. It seemed clear that Melissa had a lot of
good ideas and foresight. That was why Gus considered her the best hand he'd ever had. But what
had Gordon contributed? Had he been the brawn?

An image of some hulking muscle man providing
Gus with hard labor and Melissa with stud service
sprang to mind. Travis disliked both the image and
himself for the voyeuristic nature of his thoughts.
Even so, he couldn't resist wondering, "What was
he like?"

"Who?" Melissa asked, startled by the harsh tone of Travis's question.

Travis was equally astonished. He had no idea he'd spoken out loud. He tried to cover the jealous inflection she might have heard in his voice by sounding deliberately casual, but he failed miserably. "That *good man* you were married to. Gordy. Wasn't that his name?"

Thinking Travis was displaying a disreputable attitude toward the dead, her reply was curt. "Yes. And he *was* a good man!"

Her eyes implied she had grave doubts about the goodness of the man she was presently with, and Travis knew he deserved her censure. Yet he had never felt this intense, immediate desire for a woman who was obviously still hung up on another man, even though that man was no longer alive.

It was senseless for him to begrudge Gordon Lindstrand for having known Melissa in all the ways he wanted to know her himself—beginning with the nearest haystack! How could he damn her dead husband for the legal right to do what Travis could only fantasize about? Travis had no rights where she was concerned, yet he was feeling like a betrayed husband. It was crazy!

"I'm going in," Melissa said. "The ice cream is ready to go in the freezer."

Not waiting to ask him if he planned to join her, and it was obvious that she didn't really care, Melissa disappeared into the house. Travis sat where he was, staring beyond the porch banister toward the fields.

He was filled with nostalgic memories. Wintersfield—the home of his family. It had been the one constant in his childhood, a childhood spent at one boarding school after another. With the exception of one wonderful summer, he'd only been allowed to visit Wintersfield for a few weeks at a time. How he'd cherished those short visits. It was at Wintersfield that he'd learned what it meant to be part of a family, to have roots and be unconditionally accepted.

When he'd been with his grandparents and uncle, he'd been more than a mannerly schoolboy who could boast good grades. They hadn't brought him out to impress their friends, then shipped him away again. They had allowed him to be himself. Seeing Kenny and Gus together was like seeing himself many years ago.

He understood Melissa's possessive attitude toward the farm. He felt exactly the same way. Wintersfield was in his blood, and he'd somehow felt that it would always be there waiting for him. Although he hadn't remembered before, thinking back he recalled mention of Melissa and her husband in Gus's letters. Evidently, she one day planned to own the place. Wintersfield was going to belong to somebody else, and as far as he knew there was not a thing he could do about it. He should never have waited this long before coming back.

"I DON'T WANT TO go to bed, yet," Kenny complained as Melissa ushered him up the stairs.

"We're leaving now anyway, Kenny," Gus called after them. "See you in the morning, partner."

"You can talk to Travis some more tomorrow,"

Melissa stated firmly. "The man's been hurt, honey. He needs to get his rest, too."

Kenny continued his argument all through his quick bath, but by the time Melissa had him dressed in his summer pajamas, his yawns were becoming more frequent and he was more than ready to close his eyes when she led him up to bed. Even though she knew he was very sleepy, she didn't dare skip any part of their nightly ritual. She'd tried that a couple of times and found that her young son could wake up over one misplaced teddy bear.

Patiently she lined up each stuffed animal on the shelf over Kenny's head, then bent down to bestow a kiss on his glowing pink cheek. "Sweet dreams, pie face," she whispered as she brushed her hand over his forehead, pushing back the stubborn lock of hair that refused to stay in place even when wet. *I've never seen anything like it,* she said to herself, smiling, then pictured another forehead and a sheaf of gold-streaked brown hair that fell enticingly over a deeply tanned brow.

What a stupid comparison! Her son was not anything at all like Travis Winters. Kenny was a sweet, open, dear little person, and Travis was his exact opposite! There had been a few moments on the porch when she'd felt herself drawn to him, having sensed a vulnerability in him, but he had proved himself to be completely insensitive. She couldn't wait for him to leave the farm so everything could get back to normal. She and Gus had settled down into a very comfortable routine, and she certainly didn't need Travis around to disrupt things.

She turned off Kenny's light and shut the door

behind her. She was on her way downstairs to the kitchen, intending to load their ice-cream bowls into the dishwasher, when she heard the rhythmic creak of the porch swing. She knew who was there before she stepped out on the porch to confront him. "I thought you went home with Gus."

Travis crushed out his cigarette in the freestanding ashtray. Melissa noted it wasn't the first one he'd had. She hadn't seen him smoke all evening, but judging by the pile of stubs in the tray, he'd certainly made up for it in the last hour. He must have been out here chain-smoking the whole time she had been giving Kenny a bath and putting him to bed.

"I told Gus I'd be along later," Travis said, as he stood up from the swing. "There's something I need before going to bed."

"What?" If Gus had volunteered her to provide Travis with some personal service, she'd never forgive him. Still, maybe all Travis wanted was an aspirin. Gus was notorious for being out of them, and being arthritic, he consumed them in volume.

When Travis touched the small bandage at his temple, Melissa was almost positive that that was indeed what he wanted. "Are you in a lot of pain?"

"A lot," Travis agreed, coming closer and closer to her with every slow step.

In the darkness his eyes glittered like a nighthawk's, and Melissa felt herself shiver. "I...I'll get you some aspirin," she stammered, starting back into the house, but she stopped at the sound of his low chuckle.

"Aspirin won't help the ache I have," he drawled,

the seductive inflection in his voice holding her in place.

She knew what he was after as soon as he had braced one arm on either side of the doorframe, trapping her in place. "Travis," she pleaded, but he took no notice. Tenderly he answered her plea with the lovely, shortened rendition of her name, "Lissa?"

She swallowed the huge lump in her throat. Because of his hurt ribs, she knew all she would have to do was push him away, but her arms refused to move. Travis didn't have the same problem. He clasped a determined finger and thumb around each of her wrists, then moved closer until his thighs brushed against Melissa's bare legs.

Seconds later, her wrists were in the custody of one large masculine hand. With his free hand, he placed his palm just below her throat, the ball of his thumb stroking her jaw. The feel of his calloused fingers against her soft skin so astonished her that all she could manage was a disbelieving, "Don't do this, Travis."

"This, my lovely Lissa?" He bent his head and kissed her cheek. "Or this?" His lips nibbled their way across to her ear where the tip of his tongue nuzzled the tender lobe.

She inhaled the smoky scent of his hair, the erotic musk of his skin and the heat of his breath. Although she wanted to, she couldn't pull away—his hold on her wrists keeping her his willing captive. She didn't know how to cope with him. He was so sexy, so experienced, so different from Gordy.

She didn't even like him, and yet she wanted him

to kiss her, hold her. Would it be so very wrong to let herself enjoy the feel of a man's lean, hard body pressed to her contrasting soft one? She had normal needs and desires, and there was nothing wrong in indulging them to at least a small degree, especially with someone she instinctively knew was an expert.

His thumb began massaging the side of her neck, tantalizing the tender skin just below her chin. Meanwhile his lips wandered down the side of her face to her collarbone, then explored the smooth flesh on either side of her halter strings. She thought her heart would stop as a warm, melting sensation radiated from a point in the center of her being.

There wasn't an inch of space between their bodies. The frantic beat of her heart pulsed through her fingers, and the answering thunder of his throbbed against the back of her hand. Instinctively her fingers curled, her nails digging into her palms as if to break the current that flowed between them. He felt the tension in her hands and lifted them up to his mouth.

Unable to look away, Melissa watched as he closed his teeth over one bent finger, tugging gently on each of her knuckles until first one hand was pulled open, then the other. She had always thought her large, work-worn hands unattractive, but he made love to them as if they were fashioned from the smoothest silk. It was the most delicate yet devastating form of erotica she'd ever endured.

When he bent his head to take her lips, her reaction was purely instinctive. It was all she could do not to wind her arms around his neck. She shut her eyes very tightly, trying to deny that she wanted him to kiss her as much as he wanted to. His mouth

brushed her lips, and Melissa felt a thrust of desire
so strong it frightened her. Her heart pounded so
heavily that she could feel the vibrations in her
throat. He felt them too and soothed her fears away
with the gentle stroking of his thumbs, massaging
the quivering pulse points as his tongue teased her
lips.

With a tiny aroused moan, her lips parted, and she
shuddered with unbearable frustration when his
tongue thrust into her mouth, then withdrew, over
and over again. The radiating warmth that had
coursed through her exploded into a fiery heat, first
detonated somewhere in the region of her stomach,
then shooting to the deepest, most feminine recess
where it intensified with each darting motion of his
tongue. She was oblivious to his husky growl of satisfaction, her body demanding that he stop playing
with her mouth and pay attention to the rest of her.

When he finally made a thorough claim, it was
with a slow probing of every soft crevice. She kissed
him back a little wildly, her body arching toward the
cradle of his hips. His response to her excitement
was so primitive, it was like being hit by summer
lightning.

He grasped her by the hips, pinning her between
the door and his hard body, kissing her with a savage passion that demanded her complete surrender.
Melissa moved out of the world of logic, forgot all
common sense and responded only to the masterful
conquest of his tongue, the circular movements of
his hips, his very evident arousal.

Travis's nostrils were filled with the flower-sweet
scent of her hair. The taste of her was no surprise,

but he amazed himself by needing more and more. He swallowed the little sounds she made at the back of her throat as if they were candy and he had developed an incurable sweet tooth. This was madness, but he couldn't seem to stop, not after Melissa's arms slipped around his waist and he could feel every glorious, soft inch of her pressed against him. At first the pain in his chest was not that intense, but then in her excitement she hugged him tightly and he felt as if a knife were being twisted inside.

Melissa didn't know what had happened when he suddenly released her. He was breathing hard as he tore himself away, his eyes slightly glazed. She watched with growing confusion as he brushed the unruly hair off his forehead, then pinched the tension from between his brows.

She suddenly realized what must have caused his withdrawal. "I'm sorry if I hurt you."

Travis gasped for breath, increasing his own pain when he couldn't stifle his self-derisive chuckle. Wincing, he bent his arm over his middle, bracing his injured ribs. "This has got to be a first," he grumbled disgustedly. "That's supposed to be the man's line."

He didn't see the flash of hurt cross her face and wouldn't have understood it if he had. Melissa was the only one who was aware of how threatened she'd become about her femininity. Was Travis implying that her strength had not only hurt his ribs but wounded his masculine pride?

She looked away, stiffening when he continued angrily, "Dammit! That was exactly what I was afraid of. I never should've kissed a woman like you."

Unmindful of his injuries, Melissa roughly shoved him aside and slipped into the house. "And I should never have let you!" From the other side of the screen, she glared at him, feeling no sympathy for his gasping moans. "This was a mistake that won't be repeated," she declared coldly, then slammed the storm door shut in his astonished, pale face.

WITH MITZI, Gus's tricolored English shepherd at her heels, Melissa made her way through the foggy dawn to the cow barn. She lifted her face up to the misting rain, needing the cool moisture to refresh her spirits. It was a good rain, a "farmer's rain," her father had always called it, the kind of rain that fell gently in the morning, nurturing the young plants.

Melissa clutched a thermos of coffee against her poncho-covered bosom. Gus had thrust the thermos into her hands when she'd taken Kenny over to his house just a few minutes ago. She'd be able to enjoy the fragrant brew, laced with cream and sugar, once she got the morning's chores under way.

It was the same routine every morning. She would rise before the dawn, eat a quick, light breakfast, drop Kenny off at Gus's, then go to the barn to start the morning milking. Thank God for Gus, Melissa blessed him for the thousandth time. She would never have made it through the past year if it hadn't been for the kind older man.

Kenny was far too young to leave alone in the mornings, and though he did have a few chores each day and provided some help during the milking, Melissa preferred taking him to Gus's instead of out to the barn. Throughout most of the year it was still too dark and cold to make a small child walk from the house to the barn.

Even though he had been freed of the morning milking for the past six years, Gus still rose early, claiming old habits couldn't be broken. He insisted that he enjoyed Kenny's company, but Melissa had a sneaking suspicion that Gus might have allowed himself the luxury of another hour's sleep if she hadn't needed someone to be with Kenny. Once Kenny was fully awake, he chattered nonstop and Melissa wondered just how Gus, who had led a solitary life for most of his years, could stand it.

She gave a playful pat to the silky head that kept nudging her. "Sorry, Mitzi, I forgot to say good-morning, didn't I?"

Melissa bent down to scratch the animal behind the ears, another part of the morning ritual. As soon as the dog was satisfied that she'd gotten her deserved attention, she cocked her head, waiting for Melissa's command. "Go get 'em, Mitzi." Immediately the dog sped away, crawled through the bottom slats of the wooden fence and raced across the barnyard.

The dog was Kenny's adoring companion throughout most of the day, but at milking time she was as useful as an extra hand. It was Mitzi's job to bring the cows into the barnyard. Melissa watched in never-ending admiration as Mitzi pulled unerringly at the leather thong at the gate and jumped aside as it swung open. Then, with her white-tipped tail held like a plume, Mitzi trotted toward the herd of dairy cattle. Gus had trained her well, for it didn't take her long to get the slow-moving cows started toward the barn.

Melissa flipped the lights on and turned on the master switch that started the compressors. A noisy hum filled the barn as water flooded the lines and emptied into the drinking cups in front of each stall. This done, she walked to the back door.

Her rubber galoshes made squishing noises as she trod through the muddy barnyard. Dozens of black-and-white faces greeted her there and automatically took their single-file order as soon as they spotted her. "Good morning, ladies," she called, swinging the door wide, then quickly jumping behind it as the first three-quarter-ton Holstein-Friesian strode by at a leisurely pace. As there was little to do but lean against the door and watch the animals go by, she found herself almost dozing between yawns as she stood protected behind the barn door.

It hadn't been a restful night. All she had done was think about Travis. Before yesterday, her life had been going along just fine. Then that golden-eyed devil had showed up and made her feel things she didn't want to feel, respond to his kisses in a way that made her blush just thinking about it. Her rational side knew full well the reason Travis had stopped their embrace last night. His injuries were far from healed, and her arms around his midriff had caused pain.

But why had he made that sexist remark after she'd apologized? It had made her feel like a bone-crushing woman wrestler. His final words had effectively rubbed salt into the wound. "I never should've kissed a woman like you." Had her response to his lovemaking been that unsatisfactory?

She glared at the last cow who came through the barn door. "I never asked him to do it, you know. Men! They're more trouble than they're worth."

The animal gave a sarcastic snort as if disagreeing with Melissa's assessment, and she barely waited long enough for Mitzi to trot through the barn door before slamming it shut. "What do *you* know?" she went on, berating the cows. "You gals have been out of circulation so long, you'd cow down to the first sweet-talking bull who happened along. Well, I'm made of stronger stuff, ladies."

Through the long two-aisle barn, metal clanged against metal, ringing like a blacksmith's hammer upon an iron anvil. More than one docile animal turned big brown eyes on her as she slammed their stanchions closed. "A woman like you." She couldn't stop dwelling on Travis's last remark, her state of mind becoming more agitated with each belligerent repetition.

"All men ever seem to want is some tiny piece of feminine fluff." Her retort was repeated along with the vow that he'd never get the chance to reject her again. "All us cows should just stay in the barn where we belong," she bit out, jabbing a large scoop into the feed bin. Each animal's ration of grain and high-protein mix was delivered in record time.

When she was done, tails were swishing wildly, cloven hooves were stamping as the nervous animals shifted in their stalls. "Get yourself under control, Melissa Lindstrand," she scolded herself aloud when even Mitzi raised her glossy head from her curled up position on a pile of feed bags by the door.

"Any more of this and every cow in here will dry up!" Taking deep calming breaths, she strode to the shelf holding the radio and flipped it on.

The radio was constantly tuned to the state university FM station, for it was a proven fact that production was greater when soothing music was played during milking time. Instantly the full sounds of an orchestra playing a symphony emanated from the speakers hanging from the beams. The singing of the violins backed by the heavier double basses and cellos had a calming effect on animals and human alike.

Melissa began humming along with the flutes and clarinets as she lugged a milking machine to the first station, washed the animal's udder, then swung the heavy leather strap over the cow's back. She attached the milking machine to the strap, applied the teat cups and turned on the machine. "Music, food for the soul, soothes more than the savage breast," she remarked as she repeated the process with the cow stationed across the aisle.

With two sessions of good music per day, Melissa, like many dairy farmers, was quite knowledgeable about the masters' symphonic creations. She played a game, trying to guess the composer of the piece as she readied each animal for the milking machine, and by the time the music reached its triumphant climax, she had settled on either Brahms or Schubert. "You have been listening to the Symphony in D by Franz Schubert," was the announcement just before a brief newscast. *Not bad, I'm getting better,* Melissa thought with a smile.

She proceeded down the aisle to a heifer's stall and flipped through the charts clipped to a board hanging on a post. The animal had been bred in the autumn, and if Melissa's calculations were correct, should be near delivery. The heifer seemed a bit more restless than usual, and Melissa checked for signs of freshening. They were there, and Melissa decided she'd better keep the young bovine in the barn.

There were five other pregnant animals, and after checking them, Melissa determined that another, a heifer also, might deliver within the next twenty-four hours. In all likelihood it could be a very long night, since heifers seemed to choose the wee hours to deliver and sometimes needed assistance. Melissa cursed Travis again for the sleep she'd lost the night before.

By the time she'd let out the cows, rinsed out the machinery and set the electric barn cleaner into motion, Melissa could hear her stomach rumbling. Travis or no Travis, she was ready for the big breakfast Gus would have waiting for her by now. After finishing the last of the morning's tasks, she tossed some clean straw into the two hiefers' stalls, made sure they had plenty of food and water, then left the barn.

It had stopped raining and the sun was shining brightly, improving her mood immensely. Little puffs of steam rose from the grass where the warming rays fell, and flocks of birds were prattling in the large oak trees along the walk. Her arrival beneath the spreading limbs sent the birds into motion. Sparrows, wrens and robins took to the sky in a flurry of feathered wings, only the more docile mourning doves seemed not to care that she'd intruded on their territory.

She mounted the few steps to Gus's small enclosed back porch with some trepidation, but as she pulled off her muddy boots and placed them near the door, she adjusted her attitude. She'd grown up the youngest of four children and the only daughter. Raised with three older brothers, she'd certainly had her share of teasing and knew how to hold her own. If she could deal with those three, she could certainly deal with Travis!

She hung her poncho on a hook by the door, then eyed her baggy overalls and chambray shirt. Travis had judged her unfeminine last night, and there was nothing about her to change his opinion this morning. "And you don't want him to," she reminded herself. Straightening her shoulders, she reached for the doorknob, delighted that her hand wasn't shaking.

"Did you say something, Mel?" Gus inquired from his place by the stove.

The delicious aroma of fresh sausage and pancakes caused her stomach to rumble in eagerness as she stepped farther into the kitchen. "I said it smells awfully good in here," she evaded, forcing a broad smile that became sincere when she found that Travis was nowhere to be seen.

She knew Travis hadn't left because his racy blue Corvette was still parked outside. It was probably only a temporary reprieve, since Kenny's chatter was loud enough to rouse the soundest sleeper, but any respite from his disturbing presence was welcome. "Is that Kohler's sausage?"

"Sure is," Gus affirmed as he turned the links with a pair of tongs, then concentrated on breaking eggs in a bowl. "Pour yourself a cup of coffee. My partner and I'll have this meal on in a jiffy. Then, we'll see if Frank got these sausages right this time. Last week they had too much sage in them," he grumbled.

Melissa slid into a chair and stifled a giggle. Long before Melissa had arrived at Wintersfield, Gus had been buying Frank Kohler's sausage and yet complained every time that Frank had either put in too much sage or not enough. Melissa had come to wonder if Gus kept buying that sausage in the hope that some day it would be just right. The Kohler farm wasn't far, and Frank was one of Gus's cronies. Having never been invited to the all-male weekly get-together at the Eat Shop, Melissa could only imagine the argument over the recipe that was probably repeated every week.

Since Gordy's death, Kenny had been made an honorary member of that exclusive male gathering. She'd once asked him what they talked about, and Kenny had summarized the entire conversation with one sentence. "First we talk about Mr. Kohler's sausage, then cows and stuff, then the weather." It sounded as if they operated under a rigid agenda. She surmised that Travis's arrival had been categorized under the parliamentary rules as "new business."

"Well, partner, how're those pancakes coming?" Gus asked Kenny while he poured the mixture of eggs and milk into a large skillet.

Kenny stood on a stool in front of an electric griddle placed on the counter. A spatula in hand, he kept his eyes glued to the irregular shapes before

him. "Almost done," he reported proudly, slid the
spatula under a cake and managed to flip it over
without its crumbling. From the looks of the platter
resting on the counter next to him, Melissa guessed
that Gus had made the majority of the pancakes.
Most appeared perfect, but the ones piled haphaz-
ardly on top were a little flatter, and not quite as
golden.

TRAVIS AWAKENED to the smell of fresh coffee and sausage. For an instant he wondered where he was, and
then Melissa Lindstrand's face was there behind his
eyelids, those incredible blue eyes of her accusing . . . .

"Oh, Lord." He opened his eyes and rubbed his
hand over a chin in need of a shave. Then he threw
off the sheet that covered him, feeling the pull in his
ribs. Easing slowly out of the bed, Travis walked into
the adjoining bathroom and stepped into the shower.

He'd come to Wintersfield to find a little peace, to
lick his emotional wounds and allow his broken
bones to heal, but he hadn't had a moment's rest
since he'd first clapped eyes on a grimy female farmhand with flashing blue eyes and a body he could
never tire of seeing.

Even standing under the cold, brisk spray couldn't
erase Melissa's image from his mind, the same image
he'd wrestled with all night. She had made it plain
she wouldn't let him touch her again, but that one
kiss hadn't been nearly enough. The only way he
could get her out of his system now was to take her
to bed, but she was the type who would want a commitment.

Commitment was not a word in his vocabulary. He'd lived without it all his life and didn't know if he wanted it now. On the other hand, Travis was disillusioned with his current mode of living and could see himself fitting into this pleasant setup with relative ease. In his more idealistic moments he had imagined himself with a wife, children, a home to call his own.

After the explosion, while recuperating in a Miami hospital, he'd had lots of time to think. Faced with his own mortality, he'd begun to question the restlessness that kept him searching for new challenges, ever more difficult problems to solve. He saw now that one of the main reasons he'd chosen to work for Rogers Engineering was because the firm specialized in difficult projects under way in developing countries. Though terrorist attacks were not frequent, he often worked under the threat of them occurring.

Only during his enforced rest in the hospital had he realized that, if he had died, he would have left nothing behind to substantiate his existence. Even the huge monuments of steel and cement that he'd been responsible for building would eventually crumble and be replaced. What did he have that would last? Nothing. No wife or family. No home or ties of any kind.

Perhaps if he went after Melissa, he could have all those things he'd missed out on. If he really set his mind to it, was willing to give up his gypsy life-style, was willing to take a chance, he too could have a family. She had already borne one beautiful son, and he couldn't help but wonder what her offspring would look like if he was the father. He knew he'd enjoy creating them, but what kind of parent would he make? What kind of husband? Did he have the guts to open himself to another person? To take the responsibility for someone other than himself?

Standing before the bathroom mirror, Travis sprayed a mound of shaving cream into his palm, then applied it to his face. Carefully he drew the sharp razor down his jaw. Faced with himself in the mirror, he swore under his breath. Who did he think he was kidding? The decision he thought he had to make had already been decided for him. Melissa didn't want anything more to do with him. His dilemma was purely academic, unless....

"I'M GOING TO NEED some help with this." Travis's gravelly voice rumbled down the hallway as he made his way toward the kitchen. At first, he seemed unaware that Melissa was there as he strode barefoot into the room, wearing nothing but a pair of jeans and carrying a wide piece of elastic. It looked like a waist cincher, but upon appraising Travis's lean middle, Melissa was very much aware he required no such binding. The rib belt was meant to support his ribs and would cover the ugly blue-black stain that spread down his left side and across half his abdomen. Melissa winced inwardly at the sight of the large bruise. Seeing her, Travis came to a halt in midstride. After a moment of hesitation, he walked to the table and, as if the previous night had never happened, bestowed a beatific smile upon her. "Good morning," he greeted almost musically.

Golden highlights danced in his brown eyes—

highlights Melissa had come to associate with his lighter moods. He held her gaze for a moment, as if searching for something he'd lost in their clear blue depths, and Melissa dropped her eyes pretending to concentrate on the mug of coffee she held in her hands.

Travis stood so close to her that Melissa could smell the tantalizing mixture of soap and warm skin that wafted from him. His hair was damp and combed away from his face, the recalcitrant lock that normally fell across his forehead—for once—slicked back. The bandage was missing from his temple, and the wound exposed. A red streak with small dots alongside it revealed the number of stitches that had been required to close the gash on his smooth forehead.

"Morning," she mumbled, more into the cup of coffee she lifted to her lips than to him. She hoped her tone implied disinterest rather than the stunned reaction she was experiencing at the sight of the wounds marring his half-naked body. It was the spectacle of that powerful body that caused a quivering sensation to shoot through her limbs. *Ridiculous,* she scolded herself. *You grew up with three brothers and were married for seven years. You've seen a man's body before.*

Burgeoning biceps, heavily muscled shoulders and corded forearms were potent evidence of the man's strength, but the rising pectorals and taut abdomen beneath a wealth of curling golden-tipped hair proclaimed his virility. On a primitive level, all that was female about her responded to his blatant maleness. But, despite that, there was yet another reaction. Melissa's strong nurturing instincts prompted a need to reach out and soothe the wounds he had suffered. She fought to control both instincts, sure that Travis wouldn't welcome either one, at least not from her.

Melissa concentrated on the coffee cup she held in her hands, as if the dark liquid swirling in it would erase the pictures her imagination was conjuring up of Travis lying bleeding and possibly unconscious beneath a pile of debris. She disliked the man, didn't she? So why did the evidence of his pain and the possibility that he could have been killed bother her so much? Maybe it was just too much like the images she carried of Gordy's accident, painful memories she would have forever. That had to be it. After all, the man meant nothing to her except for being a temporary irritant.

Travis shouldn't have been surprised by her unenthusiastic greeting, but nevertheless it irritated him. He had his work cut out for him, all right. Hiding his displeasure, he turned to Gus, giving her his back, not wanting her to know that the more distant she behaved, the more he wanted her.

He had always prided himself on his remarkable control. "Keep everything light," was his motto. "Never let a woman know that she has any kind of power over you." Melissa Lindstrand, however, could embarrass him with one casual look from her cornflower-blue eyes. He'd have to be very careful around her. He urgently hoped that the damning evidence of his arousal would go unnoticed, and was grateful for the stiff denim of his brand-new jeans.

At first, Melissa was relieved when Travis turned his back on her. It was difficult to be so closely confronted by his gorgeous chest, but she soon found that the rear view was equally as tantalizing. His jeans were so snug that she could see the beginning of a slight indentation between his tight male buttocks. Her temperature soared beyond all control when the twin muscles bunched and relaxed right before her spellbound eyes. Her throat went dry, and the coffee in her mouth went down the wrong way, setting off a paroxysm of coughing.

"Are you all right, Lissa?" Travis stepped behind her quickly and clapped her on the back.

Melissa was glad she had a decent excuse for her red face. Sometimes, being fair-skinned was a real trial. With tears streaming from her eyes, she tried to regain her breath. The feel of Travis's hand stroking between her shoulder blades delayed her recovery. By the time she was able to talk again, all three males in the room had gathered around her. "I swallowed wrong," she croaked unnecessarily.

"Okay now?" Travis's tender murmur teased the soft shell of her ear, sending an erotic reverberation down the entire length of her spine. It was all she could do to keep from squirming off the chair.

Why did this man continue to have this effect on her? He'd already shown her that he'd run out of interest. Her mind recoiled at the thought of responding to a man who found her so lacking, but her body seemed to have other ideas. Beneath the loose chambray shirt, her breasts felt tight, swelling painfully against her constricting bra. She had never been so grateful for the stiff denim bib that covered her chest. She resisted the impulse to cross her legs as a glowing warmth spread through her loins.

Feeling more self-conscious than she ever had in her life, Melissa waved away their concern. "I'm all right. Really."

Taking her at her word, Gus and Kenny went back to making breakfast. Travis hovered behind her for a few moments, then walked away, mumbling something she didn't quite hear because she was still clearing her throat. Completely recovered, she was about to get up to refill her coffee cup when Travis suddenly reappeared, coffeepot in hand.

"You'll have to pour this yourself," he informed ruefully, setting the pot down on the table. "I still can't manage something even this simple." It was very difficult for him to admit his weakness in front of her. No wonder, she didn't care for him, he thought. So far, he'd come across as a belligerent cripple, and at the rate he was going it might take him forever to get her to change that opinion.

His unsupported ribs started to throb, and seeing that Melissa was the only possible volunteer left to help him, he forced himself to swallow another huge chunk of his pride. "Could you help me with this? I can't get the damned thing on by myself."

"No!" Melissa blurted, then felt like an idiot. She had refused a simple request prompted by nothing but need, just because she couldn't bear to touch him. "I...I mean I've never...I wouldn't know how to...ah...." Her voice trailed off in desperation as she looked around for help. "Gus, you'd better do it."

Keeping his back turned, Gus continued scooping

eggs and sausages from the skillet. "My fingers are so stiff this morning, I'd probably take half the day trying to get him fastened. You do it."

Travis watched the play of emotions on Melissa's face. He'd begun to feel like a leper until he noted the wild flare in her eyes as she struggled to keep them away from his bare chest. The lady was as turned on by him as he was by her! He noticed the agitated motion of her breasts beneath their layers of covering as she defensively crossed her arms in front of her. Suddenly Travis was filled with a joyful surge of hope. It was hard for a true blonde to contain a blush, and the sight of her rosy cheeks delighted him.

With a grin of pure enjoyment, he dangled the rib belt over the table in front of her. In his most seductive tone, he drawled, "I think you've been drafted, Lissa."

5

KNOWING SHE HAD NO CHOICE, Melissa was determined to get through this ordeal as quickly as possible. After all, it was a job that needed doing, and she was the only person available. Looking anywhere but at his body, she took the rib belt out of his hand and stood up. "So it seems," she agreed resignedly.

Looking down at the wide piece of elastic with the dangling Velcro strips, she quickly surmised how the device worked. Holding it with one hand, she reached around him and caught the free end with her other hand. Forcing herself to adopt a purely practical and impersonal attitude toward the task, she asked, "Which side do you want it fastened on?"

Standing within the circle formed by Melissa's arms and the rib belt, Travis was tempted to drop a kiss on her forehead or at least curl his hands over her hips. Instead, he held them loosely away from his body and directed her, "On the right, please."

"That's some bruise you've got there," she remarked as she pulled the belt closed and started fastening it, ignoring the sensation of his skin and chest hair brushing against her fingertips. Feeling the heat rising on her cheeks and knowing it meant her skin was probably covered with a rosy blush, she kept her face averted from his. Hoping to camouflage her reactions with casual conversation, she inquired, "How many ribs did you break?"

"Only two, but a few more are bruised." *Keep your breathing even,* Travis ordered himself as a wisp of her silky hair brushed against his chest and her sweet, fresh scent rose to torment his senses.

"How long do you have to wear this thing?" The last fastener was smoothed in place, and she stepped away. Her question was prompted by both curiosity and the need to know whether she would have to do this for him again.

"Just a few more days. I'm a quick healer." Travis held her gaze for a moment, his eyes speaking volumes, implying that the healing of his injuries would hold some special significance for her.

"I'll finish getting dressed," Travis suddenly broke the sensual current that flowed between them. "Thanks for your help, Lissa," he said as he headed through the doorway.

Melissa stood immobile for a few seconds after Travis left the room, still shaken from the nonverbal message he had sent her. A part of her glowed in response to the caressing tone he used when he pronounced his nickname for her, and another was embarrassed that Gus and Kenny had overheard it. They might also have witnessed the intimate way Travis had looked at her. Relief swept over her when she glanced around and discovered that both Gus and Kenny had apparently had their backs turned throughout the entire exchange.

Adopting as nonchalant a behavior as possible, Melissa crossed the kitchen and helped Kenny flip the last pancake on the platter. "Looks like these are ready," she exclaimed as she picked up the platter and carried it to the table. "I can hardly wait to dig in."

"I'LL TAKE A LOOK at those heifers," Gus remarked as he cleared the table. Could be somebody'll have to stay in the barn tonight."

"Me!" Kenny volunteered, enthusiasm sparkling all over his face. "I can take my sleeping bag out there. I'll keep an eye on 'em for you."

"We'll see about that," Melissa commented non-committally but bestowed a big smile on her son. She pushed away from the table and stood up. "Right now I'd better get some work done while you help Gus with the dishes." Bending down, she opened her arms toward Kenny. "Let me give you a big kiss for those pancakes."

"Aw, mom," Kenny complained as he glanced, embarrassed, toward Travis. Still, he climbed down from his chair and went into his mother's arms. "You don't kiss Gus, and he made most of the breakfast."

Hugging him to her and planting a kiss on his cheek, Melissa explained with a twinkling grin, "You're on to me. I just used your pancakes as an excuse. Moms like to hug their little boys, even if those boys think they're getting too big for that." She held him slightly away from her, smiling down into his freckle-nosed face. "You'll just have to put up with it, sport. This mom likes to hug her kid."

She cuffed him lightly on the chin. "How about it? Are you going to give me one back?" Kenny grinned mischievously up at her and wrapped his arms in a stranglehold around her neck. "Stop, stop," Melissa protested between giggles. "Any more enthusiasm and I'll pass out."

She straightened up and headed for the back door, but her step faltered briefly when she caught a glimpse of the peculiar expression on Travis's face. There was an odd smile turning up his lips and a look of... what? Hunger? Envy? On second thought, the look was one of pain. Again the need to comfort Travis somehow spread through her, as if she should walk around the table, pull him against her and soothe away all his hurts, physical and mental.

She was sure he wouldn't appreciate her mothering. Again she reminded herself that he didn't want anything from a woman like her. He'd made that perfectly clear. But this morning, he seemed to have done an about-face. Had he changed his opinion of her, or was she merely the only available female? Somehow, she thought Travis was not the kind of man to be without female companionship for any great length of time, but no matter how long he planned to remain on the farm, she was determined not to provide the entertainment.

Still, although she wasn't very experienced at this kind of thing, she was sure he felt something for her, even if it was only physical attraction. While that might feed her ego, it wasn't enough to make her fall into his arms. But this new approach was more difficult to figure out. Travis wasn't baiting her constantly as he had at supper the night before, but he wasn't dismissing her either. Far from it. The indefinable pull that had developed instantly between them was as strong as ever. It was just that he seemed to be taking a different tack. She shrugged, not willing or able to fathom his actions or her reaction to them. Melissa had work to do.

MELISSA TOSSED A BLANKET on the barn floor, then sat, adjusting her shoulders against a hay bale. She considered throwing an empty feed sack over it to protect her from the stiff stems that poked and scratched through her thin cotton blouse. Deciding the discomfort would be an asset by helping to keep her awake, she stretched her long jean-clad legs out in front of her.

She began punching some numbers into the calculator she balanced on her knee, glad she'd brought the farm accounts out with her. It was going to be a very long night with her two expectant mothers, and since birth didn't appear imminent, she could use the time to bring the ledgers up to date. Thinking music might keep the two heifers a bit calmer as well as provide her with some enjoyment, she turned on the radio.

The university station had signed off for the night and she adjusted the dial to another FM station, one that played soft background music. She stopped her figuring long enough to enjoy a medley of Beatles' hits, surprised at how beautiful it was. Arranged for a full orchestra, even "I Want to Hold Your Hand" sounded like the finest classic. Humming softly with the music, she leaned her head back and let her mind wander to her son.

After a long, busy day, Kenny had been nearly asleep by the time she'd bathed him. She'd scooped him up and carried him over to Gus's. Thoughts of spending the night with her in the barn had been forgotten when he'd been told that "Dr. Doolittle" was being shown again on television and that he could stay up and watch it. Melissa wondered if her sleepy son had lasted through the first commercial.

Hearing a low bellow coming from one of the stalls, she capped her pen and put the account book aside. She could see both heifers from the position she'd chosen and went directly to the second stall. Calmly she unlatched the half door and let herself in, watching the animal carefully. The heifer was stirring restlessly and starting to heave herself forward. "Take it easy, girl," Melissa said as she patted the animal.

"I know how you feel, sweetheart," she commiserated. "This isn't the best part of being a female, is it?"

"Then what is?" a deep voice rumbled with amusement from the front of the stall.

"How long have you been there?" Melissa gasped as the laboring heifer butted her in the small of the back.

"Not long," Travis admitted. "You've been out here all alone for hours, and I thought you might appreciate some human company."

"Ever seen a calf born? You might change your mind about being here."

"I think I can stand it," he remarked with a sparkling grin. The overhead light glinted across his gold-streaked hair, and Melissa turned her attention away from his disturbing presence.

She ran knowing hands over the heifer's heaving belly. "Things may start happening pretty soon now," she said as much to herself and the heifer as to Travis. "Since you're here, you can give me some help. There's a pair of coveralls hanging on the wall behind you. Would you toss them to me?"

"Sure. Anything else?"

"Yes, I'll need some rubber gloves." She pointed to the row of bins on the shelves beside the door. "You should find them in the second one from the left."

"Rubber gloves?" he questioned with a slight frown.

"I'm going to have to examine her," Melissa explained. "She's been in labor for quite a while, and I want to make sure that calf is in the right position. Also, there should be a nice clean bucket in the cupboard. Pour about a cup of the antiseptic into it and fill it with water."

Without another word, Travis pushed away from the stall and left to get the items she'd requested. He returned and tossed her the overalls. She was aware of his eyes watching her every move as she stepped into the white cotton garment and pulled it up over her body, stretching her arms into the sleeves before zipping up the front. "Am I allowed in the delivery room?" he asked when she was finished.

"I don't know. We'll have to ask the mother," Melissa said, adopting a teasing tone as the safest way to deal with Travis. Holding the halter and stroking the animal's neck, she asked, "What do you think, girl? Shall we let him in?" The heifer let out a soft, moaning sound.

"Is that her answer?" Travis asked with a chuckle.

"Yep," Melissa pronounced. "She thinks we'll need your help."

"And what does the doctor say?" He let himself into the stall, carrying the requested gloves and bucket of antiseptic.

"The doctor just wants to make sure you won't pass out or anything," Melissa said as she took the gloves and slid her hands into them.

"I promise," he vowed. "Now what can I do?"

"Just hold her head still and talk to her." Melissa dipped her hand and arm into the bucket. "Try to keep her as quiet as you can. Be careful or she might bash her head into you. I don't think your chest needs any more bruising."

"You're right about that," he agreed, but gamely took hold of the halter and started patting the animal's neck. "What do I say to her?"

"Anything. She doesn't care. You could recite the alphabet as long as you do it soothingly." Melissa lifted the heifer's tail and pushed one hand and arm inside her. Her arm was immediately compressed by a powerful contraction, and Melissa waited until it passed before reaching farther. She could feel tiny hooves but wasn't sure whether they were front legs or back until the calf's tongue flicked across her fingers.

Melissa giggled and started withdrawing her arm, her progress halted again by the mother's next contraction. "What's so funny?" Travis inquired from the heifer's head. "I was just telling her what pretty eyes she has."

"That's not why I was laughing. You're doing fine," Melissa assured. "The calf licked my fingers." She laughed a little harder, and Travis gave a deep chuckle. "It's in the right position, so all we have to do is make sure the mother doesn't have any trouble delivering.''

The humor left Travis's face and was replaced by a look of genuine concern. "Do you expect any?"

"You never know the first time around. She's a little small and the calf feels pretty big." Melissa pulled off the gloves and started for the door.

"Wait a minute! You're not going to leave me alone with her, are you?" His inquiry was tinged with something close to panic.

Pure mischief sparkled from Melissa's eyes as she looked back over her shoulder at him. "Just keep up the good work, nurse. Keep talking to her and most of all stay calm. I'm going next door to check on my other patient."

"This animal have a name?" he called after her.

"She's number one twenty-four." Melissa called back as she rinsed off the gloves at the old sink she'd had installed next to the cupboards.

"No wonder she's nervous. Poor thing doesn't even have a decent name."

Melissa let herself into the next stall, separated by a wooden wall from the one where she'd left Travis. The second heifer wasn't quite as agitated, and as Melissa gave her a superficial examination, it appeared that she wasn't nearly as far along as the first one. She almost laughed as she heard Travis talking to his charge.

"How about I call you Carla? You've got such big, beautiful eyes, Carla Cow. Now be a good girl and don't cause us any trouble. Anyone with gorgeous brown eyes like yours can't possibly be any trouble, can she?'' He continued with his nonstop compliments until Melissa had to cover her mouth with one hand to keep from breaking up. Travis seemed so urbane and sophisticated, yet here he was in the middle of the night, practically wooing a nervous heifer. Maybe she'd been wrong about him.

After breakfast, Melissa had been kept busy in the far reaches of the farm all day and she hadn't seen Travis again until supper. She'd been back at the house only long enough to grab a sandwich at lunchtime, and he'd been nowhere around either house. Neither had Kenny, and according to Gus, Travis had taken her son for a ride in the flashy Corvette and they were expected back at any minute. She hadn't waited around for their return.

During the evening meal, Kenny had been bubbling over with excitement about the car and spending the day with his new idol. The object of worship had been markedly quiet during the meal, and when Kenny and Gus had once again volunteered to do the evening milking Travis had gone along with them. Melissa had had some welcome hours to herself in the house. It had given her a chance to get the dishes done, as well as a few loads of laundry. She'd even gone out on the porch, propped her feet up and read the newspaper in between filling and emptying the washer and dryer.

When the milking had been finished, the trio of males had returned, but Gus and Travis had stayed only long enough to invite Kenny to watch a TV movie. She'd felt Travis's glittering eyes on her throughout supper and again when he'd brought

Kenny back, but he hadn't tormented her with teasing remarks or challenging looks, sticking to the behavior he'd adopted at breakfast.

Melissa was just leaving the adjoining stall when she heard Travis's nervously pronounced call. "Lissa! I think something's happening in here."

In a flash, Melissa was in the stall and beside the heifer. The animal was straining and bellowing with each contraction. "Won't be long, now," Melissa pronounced. "Unless this mama needs some help, her baby's going to be here in a few minutes. Easy, girl," Melissa crooned as she ran her hand along the heifer's black-and-white-patterned side, feeling the beginnings of another contraction. "That's it, sweetheart, push," Melissa coaxed as if the animal understood.

The animal labored heavily but with no result. "I'm going to have to go in and help her," Melissa explained. "I'll stay with her if you'll go get a rope for me. The one I want should be coiled up in the same cupboard where you found the gloves. It should have a little noose on one end." Travis left immediately. "Bring the gloves back, too."

The animal's straining and bellowing increased, and Melissa tried as best she could to keep her fairly calm. Without a word, she pulled on the gloves Travis held, dipped her hands into the antiseptic solution and, rope in hand, reached inside the heaving heifer. "Come on, baby, keep your feet still. I want to help you." The calf's forelegs kept slipping out of the noose every time Melissa managed to get it around them. Finally she got it fastened.

"Wind this around that support post and bring

the end back to me," Melissa ordered as she tossed the rope to Travis. He followed her command but gave her a questioning look. "I'm going to have to yank it out. You just keep mama as quiet as you can. She's not going to like this."

Melissa grasped the rope and waited for the next contraction. When it came she pulled with all her strength, leaning backward and bracing her heels in the gutter to keep from sliding forward. Hand over hand, she reeled the rope toward her, keeping the calf from slipping back at the end of the contraction. "Come on," she gritted. "Just a little farther."

Melissa felt herself being pulled forward and tried to throw all her weight against it. Suddenly she felt a strong arm wrap around her middle. Travis leaned backward with her. Their combined weight was all that was needed. Tiny hooves emerged, then a pink muzzle.

In another second, the new little calf's entire head appeared. As the rest of the animal was born, the resistance ceased and Melissa and Travis landed in a heap on the floor of the stall. For several moments, they couldn't move from their half-sitting, half-lying positions. Both were overcome by exertion and wonder over the new life that lay curled up on the clean straw.

"Look at that," Travis said in quiet awe. His breath blew warm and moist against her nape as he spoke, sending little shivers down her spine, but Melissa didn't want to shift her body away . . . at least not yet. The hostility and wariness she'd felt around Travis was relaxed as they shared the moment, his arms still locked securely around her middle.

"It's beautiful," Travis murmured. "You've got a beautiful baby, Carla. You're some doctor, Lissa."

Melissa relaxed against Travis, her breath still coming in heavy pants. "Thanks," she managed between gulps of air. "You're some nurse."

"My pleasure," he remarked, propping his chin on her head.

His armlock hadn't lessened and Melissa squirmed uncomfortably, recovered enough from the emotions and exertion wrought by the birth to want to put some distance between them. "Uh ... you can let go of me now. I need to get the noose off."

He let her go, and as she got to her feet, she heard him catch his breath. She turned back to him, a frown furrowing her brows when she saw him holding his chest and taking halting breaths. "Are you all right? Did you get hurt when I fell on you?"

Melissa knelt back down in the straw and placed her hand on his shoulder. "You shouldn't have done it, Travis. You've just hurt yourself all over again and it's my fault."

"No, it's not. I wanted to help. Believe me, I'll be all right in a minute." He lifted his face to hers, managing a rather lopsided grin. "It's a nice change to have somebody worry about me, though." He placed the tips of two fingers between her brows. "Don't frown, pretty lady. I'm okay."

His touch and the warmth of his gaze were doing wild things to Melissa's pulse rate, but she still wasn't appeased. "Are you sure? I really bashed into you, and I'm no featherweight."

"I can handle a whole lot of woman," he quipped, and his grin broadened to a bold smile. Seeing by her blush that she wasn't prepared to deal with his remark, he went on in a milder tone, "Anything else need to be done here, doctor?"

She looked over her shoulder. "Carla" was licking her newborn, effectively cleaning it and massaging it with her large, rough tongue. The little animal arched its back and struggled to its feet. The noose came off, and the calf tottered on big-kneed, wobbly legs, toward its mother.

"Mother and child are doing fine," Melissa pronounced with tear-glazed eyes. It was always such a miracle when new life came into the world, all perfectly formed and instinctively guided in those first few moments. "I don't think we're needed anymore. Look."

"How about that," Travis echoed her feelings, his smile revealing his flashing white teeth. Were his eyes just a little brighter, too? Melissa suspected, with ample proof, that worldly Travis Winters had been just as moved by the miracle as she.

The calf was already enjoying its first meal and the new mother was standing, calmly swishing her tail as if nothing unusual had happened. "All we have to do is sketch its markings. I'm so glad it's a heifer," she pronounced, and started out of the stall.

Travis was right behind her. "Got something against us males?"

"No," she replied, giggling. "You have your uses, but this is a dairy farm and we need females for the herd." She glanced into the other stall as she passed on her way to the sink. The other heifer was still quite calm. It might be several hours before she delivered.

"But don't you need some males to expand the herd?" Travis persisted.

"Nope. We use artificial insemination," she explained as she pulled off the gloves and splashed some cool water on her face.

"Doesn't sound like much fun for either the cow or the bull."

You stepped into that one, Melissa, she thought as she splashed a little more water on her face, then buried her reddened cheeks into a paper towel. Discussing artificial insemination didn't bother her; it was the silky caress of Travis's voice as he made the last statement and the fact that he was standing so close to her. It was too warm, suddenly, and she turned away from Travis, unzipped the coveralls and stepped out of them.

"Well, thanks for your help, Travis," she started, keeping the agitation out of her voice. "You don't need to hang around here. It'll probably be hours before the next one comes." *Just go,* she thought. *You're driving me crazy standing there in your tight jeans and muscle-hugging shirt.*

"Are you trying to get rid of me?"

Yes! "Of course not. I just thought you might get terribly bored out here, and there's no reason for two of us to lose a night's sleep."

"Lissa...." He placed his hands on her shoulders and gently turned her around. "I'm going to lose sleep anyway."

"Why?" Melissa asked guilelessly, looking into his eyes.

"You," he murmured, then lowered his face to hers. His lips covered her startled mouth, and his hands pulled her closer. His tongue brushed languidly back and forth across her lips, but she refused to open to him, refused to invite him inside. He lifted his head, his gaze perplexed.

"After last night, why do you want to kiss me?" Melissa got out agitatedly.

"Last night? What do you mean?"

"You said you shouldn't have kissed a woman like me. Nothing has changed since then. I'm still the same woman."

Travis read the reproach in her eyes and let out a ragged sigh. "You're right, and that's why kissing you bothered me so much. I didn't want to enjoy kissing you, but I did, and now I'm afraid I want much more from you than you're ready to give."

Melissa's heart did a frantic leap inside her chest. The look on his face verified his words. He did desire her—he wanted to make love to her—and a portion of her brain that should have resisted seemed to have shut down.

"Let me kiss you," Travis pleaded gruffly. "Let me show you how I feel," he moaned. Then his tongue plunged inside her mouth, twirling around her tongue, then guiding it into his own mouth.

Unable to hold herself back, Melissa returned his moist caress, coyly parrying his thrusts and hesitantly following his lead. She felt her hands being guided to his neck, and she had buried her fingertips in the thick hair of his nape. She loved the feel of it, the feel of him.

Eagerly his hands moved from her shoulders and covered her breasts. His lips moved across her cheek and down her throat, and the tip of his tongue made

moist circles across the rise of her breasts as his
fingers loosed the buttons of her shirt. "I need to
touch you," he murmured urgently.

Melissa wanted to protest but couldn't against the
onslaught of his mouth and fingers. One of his
hands reached around her and unfastened her bra,
and in one motion her shirt and undergarment were
tossed to the barn floor. Her whole body began to
throb as his mouth closed around a nipple and a
rough palm covered the other. Her convictions not to
provide entertainment for him were losing strength
with each caress. Melissa's body clamored for relief
from the tension that had grown since their first
meeting, and she swayed on unsteady legs into the
support of his strong body, "Travis," she pleaded
breathlessly.

Placing a series of kisses on her breasts, chest and
throat, he straightened, then swept his arm around
her. The buttons of his shirt made sharp indenta-
tions into the softness of her breasts, and the loose,
knitted weave rasped against her nipples, heighten-
ing their sensitivity as he moved against her.

"Lissa," he rasped again before covering her mouth
once more. There was no tender coaxing this time but
an insistent taking as his tongue filled her. Melissa
took a step backward but he followed, his thighs
brushing against hers as she unconsciously backed
away. Slowly he released her, then gently pushed
down on her shoulders.

It was then she realized he'd been edging her toward the blanket that she'd so innocently provided.
Some shred of reason cautioned her to push him
away, stop this seduction, but when her hands

closed over the warm solidity of his broad shoulders and his mouth sought hers again, she was clinging to him. They went down to the blanket together.

Melissa welcomed the weight of him, shuddered with exquisite sensation when he settled himself between her thighs, pressing his loins against hers. "So soft...so warm..." he whispered against the curve of her shoulder. He braced himself on his forearms and in a slow, sensual rhythm pressed, then withdrew his lower body from hers, teasing her until her thighs gripped his and held him still. She could feel the hardened heat of his virility even through the twin layers of denim that separated them from complete intimacy. Melissa shivered beneath him, arching up to meet him.

"Yes...oh, yes, Lissa," Travis growled, heaving himself slightly away and tearing off his shirt.

He came down on her, and Melissa spread her hands across his shoulders, following the indentation of his spine with her fingertips. At the feel of the rib belt, she froze, then tried to move away from him. "Travis...?"

"Mmm, keep...saying...my name." He punctuated his words with kisses leading down her throat.

"Travis!"

He stopped and raised a puzzled face to hers. "What?"

"Your ribs. We can't...I mean...you'll be hurt."

"Let me worry about it," he soothed, and began the onslaught of kisses again. Melissa shrank away.

Reason had returned to lift the sensual veil that had clouded her judgment. "No! I can't risk it."

Gingerly Travis rolled off her, his breath coming

in labored gasps as he lay on his back beside her. "Why?" His tone wasn't angry, but confused.

"It's wrong."

"Nothing that we both want this much could possibly be wrong. Try again."

Melissa moved off the blanket and reached for her bra and shirt. Slipping the garments back on, she turned to him. "Travis, I...we hardly know each other and...you don't understand."

"Understand what?"

"This is a straitlaced community. It hasn't caught up with modern times. I wouldn't be able to hold my head up in society if there was the slightest hint that I was having an affair with anyone. For Kenny's sake, I have to hold on to my reputation."

"You'd deny your own needs because you're afraid of what the neighbors might say?" A look of irritation came over his face. "What you and I do together is no one's business but our own."

"Fine." She saw he was not going to buy that excuse. "This is my own decision. I'm not getting involved with a man I hardly know."

Melissa wasn't willing to expose an even more important reason for drawing away. She couldn't face the pain of rejection, the disgust that would no doubt be in his eyes after he had made love to her. It was far safer to let him think she had a Victorian morality.

"All right," he surprised her by agreeing. "I'll admit you hardly know me, but I know enough about you to know that you're the most desirable, loving woman I've ever met."

Melissa glowed in the unexpectedly lovely tribute

but it was too late to change her mind. Nonetheless, she believed he truly meant what he said. It was exhilarating to know that such an urbane man considered her desirable.

Travis sat up and reached for his shirt. "I'll accept your 'no' for now, but you won't say it for long."

Melissa finished buttoning her shirt and tucked the tails into her jeans. "You really are impossible," she said, smiling.

"No, I'm easy." He shot her a grin that melted her insides. "And I'll also admit that you're a temptation I can't seem to ignore. I really want to prove to you that this is the best part of being a woman." He shrugged his shoulders and smiled. "Must be the devil in me."

"Maybe you should try exorcising that devil, Travis," she suggested, unable to prevent herself from sounding a bit pious. "We can't always have what we want. It's a very selfish attitude to have."

His eyes held hers levelly. "It's better than—"

A loud bellow from the first stall interrupted him. Travis swiftly completed buttoning his shirt. "Come on, doctor." He grabbed hold of her hand. "This nurse has learned enough tonight to know there's another baby on the way!"

6

IT WAS FOUR DAYS LATER when Melissa placed Kenny's small suitcase in the trunk of her Buick sedan. Walking around the car, she got in and inserted the key. It was a warm morning, and the car was stuffy inside, so she rolled down the window. After taking a deep breath of fresh air, she turned to her son who was fidgeting on the front seat. She smiled to cover her annoyance. "Look, honey. Grandma and grandpa are really looking forward to having you and your cousins stay with them. You wouldn't want to hurt their feelings, would you?"

Kenny stared down at his shiny dress shoes for a moment, frowned, then finally voiced why he'd had such a downcast face all morning. "No, but Travis said he was going to teach me to ride a bike today. He said to come over right after church."

"What bike?" Melissa asked as she reached down to turn on the ignition. She backed out of the garage and turned the car around in the driveway.

"The one in Gus's garage. It's old, but it's better than my tricycle. I'm too big to ride a baby's bike." Kenny squared his small shoulders and sat up straight, as if to show how much he'd aged recently. "Travis says he was five when he learned how to ride a big bike. I'm five, too."

Melissa gritted her teeth. Ever since his arrival, there had been very few conversations between herself and Kenny that hadn't contained a "Travis says" this or a "Travis says" that. "You'll still be five when you get home," she assured. "You know that grandpa was planning to take you to see the animals at Como Park today. We arranged this two weeks ago, Kenny. You also know that Sunday is the only day he'll be able to go. It's hard for a farmer to snatch some time away from his work, but grandpa really wants to take you and your cousins to the zoo. You can learn how to ride a bike anytime, can't you?"

"But I'm gonna be gone a whole week. What if Travis leaves before I get back home?"

"Somehow, I don't think he will," Melissa remarked dryly as she stopped the car in front of Gus's house and gave two short beeps on the horn. She might wish that Travis would pack up and go, but she saw no signs of that happening. Indeed, it seemed as if every time she turned around he was there, his dark eyes filled with intimate challenge, a challenge that was becoming more and more difficult to withstand.

After that passionate interlude in the barn, she feared it was only a matter of time before she succumbed to his potent brand of male charm. More than anything, she hoped he would leave before that happened. He seemed enamored of their slow-paced life-style, but how long would it last? Right now, the farm was serving as a kind of rest home for him, but she wasn't planning to be part of his rest and relaxation.

Although he'd told her that his injured ribs felt much better and the wound on his forehead looked entirely healed, he'd made no mention of going back to work. He had a good job that assuredly paid him very well. He'd have to return to it soon, wouldn't he? "Well, if Travis does have to go, I can teach you to ride."

From the disgusted look on Kenny's face, she could tell that her suggestion wasn't well received. "I can ride no-handed."

Kenny was still dubious.

"I'll bet I can pop a wheely better than Travis."

"Gee, mom. Can you really do a wheely?"

From the incredulity in Kenny's tone, the size of his widened blue eyes, it appeared she had just climbed up several rungs on her son's ladder. Melissa smiled and snapped her fingers. "Like that," she bragged, "nothing to it."

"Wait till I tell Travis," Kenny stated in an awed voice.

"Tell me what, old man?" Travis inquired as he opened the car door, gestured Kenny to move over, then lowered himself onto the front seat.

"Never mind, Kenny." Melissa spoke before her son could answer, hoping Travis wouldn't notice the twin spots of pink dotting her cheeks. "Gus didn't say you were going to church with us this morning, Travis."

It was all she could do not to visibly react when Travis lifted his arm and slid it across the back of the seat. His fingers came to rest only a few inches from her right shoulder. "I thought it might do me some good," he remarked earnestly. "I haven't forgotten that sermon you gave me the other day."

For a heart-stopping moment he held her gaze, his dark eyes crinkling at the corners and a devilish grin turning up his lips. He took a swift inventory of her floral-print skirt and white short-sleeved blouse, lifting one brow at the sight of her fragile swiss-lace hose and dainty sling-back pumps. There was nothing repentant about him, and they both knew it.

"I think attending church does everyone some good," she said righteously.

The "even you" was implied, but he heard it and chuckled. "Then let's go. Gus said the service started at ten and...." He glanced at his watch. "It's a quarter to already."

"Isn't Gus coming?" Melissa swiveled her head to stare at the back door of the house. "He's not sick, is he?"

"His arthritis is acting up a bit, that's all," Travis assured her quickly. "I told him to take a couple of his pills and stay in bed this morning."

Although Melissa wasn't comfortable with Travis without Gus around to serve as a buffer, she had to agree that Travis had done the right thing. Some days Gus had so much pain in his legs he could hardly walk. A few more hours of rest would probably do him a world of good, give his medicine a chance to work. Besides, there was Kenny. Surely Travis would behave himself in front of her son. In church he wouldn't dare do anything to embarrass her, would he?

"Want me to drive?" Travis asked when it looked as if they weren't going anywhere.

"No way," Melissa said crossly. "I've seen how you drive. We're going to church, not the Indianapolis 500."

"At least I'd get us there on time. At this rate we might have to use up a few of our Sunday prayers just to get you out the driveway."

"I'm going." The gears ground together as Melissa put the car into first and stepped on the gas. She had never been so glad that their farm was only a few miles out of town. Today it was going to seem like a hundred.

Once she was on the main road, she concentrated on her driving, listening to Kenny's chatter with only half an ear. Out of the corner of her eye, she glanced at Travis. He was wearing an obviously tailor-made, blue pin-striped suit, a white dress shirt with French cuffs and a beautiful silk tie. The gold-and-pearl cuff links must have cost him the earth!

He was going to stick out like a very urbane sore thumb in the small community church. She could almost hear the local matrons speculating about him. Where on earth did Mel find a man like that? Do you suppose he's interested in her? Looks like she's made quite a good catch. She pictured a small blond dynamo with shrewd eyes. Mother! Elaine Kvam would be the worst of the lot. Melissa was unaware of her resigned sigh as she began praying. *Please, Lord, don't let mom start matchmaking.*

"What's the matter, mommy?" Kenny asked. "You're not wearing the right face."

"Nothing's the matter," Melissa said with amazing calm, not daring to look at Travis. She didn't quite understand her son's comment. "This is the only face I own, honey. It follows me everywhere."

"No, it's not," Kenny qualified, and she wished

she'd let the matter drop as soon as he continued, "When you're mad at me, you wear your growly face. If you get all your work done and the cows give a lot of milk, you wear a smiley face. Sunday mornings you wear a kinda angel face and sing all the time. Right now, you look sorta growly. Are you mad at me?"

Melissa could feel the vibrations of Travis's suppressed laughter through the car seat. "I'm not mad at anyone, Kenny. I'm sorry if you thought so." She smiled at him. "Is that better?"

"Much more angelic," Travis remarked, agreeing with Kenny's nod. While Melissa struggled to keep her smile in place, Travis dropped his arm around Kenny's shoulder. "Okay, fella, what were you going to tell me when I got in the car?"

Immediately Melissa's face turned "growly" but neither of her loquacious passengers seemed to notice. "Look Kenny. There's grandpa's car coming down Main Street."

"Uh-huh," Kenny muttered with all the interest of a block of cement. "My mom says she can pop a wheely better than you, Travis. Do you think she can?"

Melissa made an unnecessarily sharp turn into the church parking lot, then another into the first available space. When the car screeched to a sudden halt, its two other occupants were pressed up against the door.

"Not the Indianapolis 500, you said," Travis quipped sardonically as he gently pried Kenny away from his still-sore ribs.

It took Melissa several moments to get herself

mentally prepared for her upcoming trial. Travis, on the other hand, showed a surprising amount of excess energy as he swiftly got out of the car and walked around to her side before she had made the conscious decision to move. By the time her hand came down on the handle, he had gallantly opened her door. "Come on, angel face. The church bells are ringing."

Angel face! Her cheeks felt hotter than burning brimstone, a substance that would definitely not be found in heaven. She glowered up into a pair of twinkling brown eyes, wishing to ring one more bell—his!

As gracefully as possible, she shifted her legs out of the car, amazing herself by allowing Travis to assist her without taking a swing at him. "Kenny?" she called, not seeing her son anywhere.

"He ran off to say hello to his grandparents." Travis pointed to the opposite end of the tree-lined parking lot where Kenny was waiting beside a battered-looking blue Chevy.

"Oh, fine," Melissa muttered under her breath. She had hoped not to meet up with her mom and dad until the service was over. There had been a chance she could have gotten lucky and avoided making introductions altogether. She might have been able to dispatch Travis back to her car while she transferred Kenny's things to her parents' car.

With a sinking heart, she watched Kenny pull on her father's hand, urging him to start walking toward her and Travis. Although her father stood well above six feet tall and weighed over two hundred pounds, the little boy had no trouble moving him.

Her mother, looking deceptively fragile and very pretty in a peach-colored dress, followed quickly behind. "Damn and blast. Here they come." She didn't realize she had spoken out loud until Travis laughed.

"Lissa!" he berated softly, taking her arm. "Do you think this is an appropriate place to start swearing? That is a church over there, you know."

Hadn't she known that one day her habit of talking to herself would get her into trouble? She tried to pull her arm away, but Travis had taken a very firm grip. She could feel his fingers burning on the bare skin above her elbow.

"Don't you like your parents?" he asked.

"Of course I do." Even though they were still a considerable distance away, Melissa could already see a speculative sparkle in her mother's blue eyes. She might look like a harmless, diminutive lady, but Melissa knew she had the personality of a five-star general. She'd put her mother up against Travis's father any day of the week without having the slightest doubt who would come out on top. After years of experience, Melissa still had trouble standing up for herself with the woman, or convincing her mother that she intended to control her own life. "You're going to regret this. You don't know my mother."

"What's wrong with her?" Travis began propelling her forward, returning Kenny's wave with his free hand. When they were close enough to her parents that they might be overheard, Travis leaned close to her and whispered in her ear. "She looks okay to me."

"Oh, for heaven's sake!" Melissa said under her breath. "Let's get this over with."

"Fear not, angel face. I'm right beside you," Travis assured softly, deliberately misunderstanding her continued reluctance. His fingers slid down her arm and grabbed hold of her hand. "If the going gets tough, we'll simply make a run for it."

"Morning, Melissa," Kenneth Kvam greeted, his piercing blue eyes fixed on Travis. "And you must be Gus's nephew." He thrust out his bearlike hand.

Travis let go of Melissa in order to return the handshake, and she felt as if her fingers had suddenly been freed from a steel vise. She hoped Travis was now learning what that feeling was like, but when she glanced over at his face, expecting to see him covering a wince, all she saw was an easy smile.

Squaring her shoulders, she gave in to the inevitable. "Mom, dad, this is Travis Winters. Travis, my parents, Kenneth and Elaine Kvam."

As soon as the pleasantries were over, the going got even tougher than Melissa had expected. "Hold my arm, Kenneth," Elaine began as they approached the pitted sidewalk that led up a steep grassy knoll. "Melissa, you'd better hold on to Travis. I don't know why they had to build the church on top of a hill. It's so hard to get up this incline in high heels, especially when you're not used to wearing them. Wasn't it about this time last year when you fell down and sprained your ankle, dear?"

That's right, mom, Melissa grimaced. *Point out to the man that I'm something of a klutz.* Out loud, she merely said, "I can't really remember."

In an admirable show of gallantry, Travis held out

his arm, and knowing her mother wouldn't budge an inch until her daughter had taken her advice, Melissa took a light hold of his elbow. She made no comment when Travis reached for her fingers and firmly pulled her arm through his.

"Watch your step," he advised politely as they began walking.

"Tell us all about yourself, Travis." Elaine's friendly smile implied that the statement was made out of polite curiosity, but Melissa recognized an order when she heard one. Glad not to be the current victim of her mother's third-degree questions, Melissa's step became considerably lighter. As long as her mother didn't attempt any matchmaking, she was perfectly content.

Poor Travis! He had thought he was going to church, not the Spanish Inquisition. Elaine plied him with personal questions every step of the way up the hill. By the time they reached the front steps of the church, she had found out exactly what Travis did for a living, what kind of salary he brought down, how he'd hurt himself, and what steps he planned to take to eliminate such accidents in the future.

Travis gave Melissa a look that said, *I see what you mean. Help me!* and she returned it with one that said *Sorry, it's each man for himself.* A small crowd of parishioners had gathered in front of the church, and although Melissa normally didn't take part in the weekly exchange of local gossip, she decided to make an exception this morning.

Feeling somewhat like a rat about to desert a sinking ship, she said, "I see an old friend of mine over there, and I'd like to say hello. Mom, why don't you take Kenny and Travis in with you? I'll join you as soon as I've said a few words to Maggie Birch. I haven't talked to her since her last baby was born."

Melissa didn't enter the church until she was sure that her parents were already seated. It would be a simple matter to slip into their pew when the service was ready to start and there was no longer any chance for conversation. She would also make sure she sat next to Kenny or her father. Maybe it was a good thing her folks had come along. Now she didn't have to spend an entire hour sitting beside Travis, trying to ignore the inquiring looks from her neighbors.

She didn't know how Travis had accomplished it, but he had managed to extricate himself from her mother's clutches and stood waiting for her in the church vestibule. His expression was grim, but he made no comment as he reached for her arm. A moment later, the organ began playing the opening hymn.

"Where are we sitting?" she whispered.

"Over there," he whispered back. He didn't point but started escorting her. Taking a steely grip on her elbow, he pulled her along beside him until he found two empty spaces in a pew halfway up the side aisle.

"We're supposed to sit with my folks," she insisted softly, craning her neck to locate her parents. "Kenny and I sit with them every Sunday."

"I asked your mother if she wouldn't mind taking Kenny in with her while I waited for you." He lifted a heavy black hymnal from the wooden holder

Harlequin Temptation™

Have you ever thought
you were in love
with one man...only
to feel attracted to another?

Exclusive Harlequin home subscriber benefits!

- CONVENIENCE of home delivery
- NO CHARGE for postage and handling
- FREE *Harlequin Romance Digest*®
- FREE BONUS books
- NEW TITLES 2 months ahead of retail
- A MEMBER of the largest romance fiction book club in the world

GET **FIRST IMPRESSIONS** FREE AS YOUR INTRODUCTION TO *Harlequin Temptation*™ PLUS A FREE TOTE BAG!

 ® No one touches the heart of a woman quite like Harlequin

YES, please send me FREE and **without obligation** my *Harlequin Temptation* romance novel, *First Impressions* and my FREE tote bag. If you do not hear from me after I have examined my FREE book, please send me 4 new *Harlequin Temptation* novels each month as soon as they come off the press. I understand that I will be billed only $1.75 per book (total $7.00). There are no shipping and handling or any other hidden charges. There is no minimum number of books that I have to purchase. In fact, I may cancel this arrangement at any time. The FREE tote bag and *First Impressions* are mine to keep as a free gift, even if I do not buy any additional books.   142 CIX MDC6

Name

Address   Apt. No.

City   State/Prov.   Zip/Postal Code

Signature (If under 18, parent or guardian must sign.)

This offer is limited to one order per household and not valid to present *Harlequin Temptation* subscribers. We reserve the right to exercise discretion in granting membership. Offer expires June 30, 1985.   PRINTED IN U.S.A

Get this romance novel and tote bag
FREE as your introduction to

Harlequin Temptation ™

◁ See exciting details inside.

carved out of the pew in front of them, began shuffling through the pages, then murmured, "I'm still giving thanks that she was so delighted to let me stay behind."

Melissa's "Oh, no," was loud enough to call attention to herself and the befuddled-looking man who stood beside her staring into her hunted blue eyes. She covered her embarrassment and diverted his attention by pointing to the correct stanza in the hymn that everyone else in the congregation had already begun singing. Giving Travis a sharp nudge with her elbow, she prompted him to open his mouth while she did the same.

She kept on singing until she was certain there was nobody still looking at her, then leaned closer to Travis and whispered in his ear. "You idiot! You don't know what you've just gotten us into."

During the next chorus, he breathed back, "What *are* you talking about?"

There was no chance to answer him until the offering plates were being passed and everyone else's attention was fixed on finding their donation envelopes.

"This is a very small town," she whispered. "Sitting alone together in church is almost like making a public declaration of intent." She smiled at the usher, nodded a silent hello to Maggie Birch's beaming grandmother who was seated in the pew across from them, then kept her eyes firmly glued on the printed bulletin that outlined the progression of the morning service.

During Pastor Halvorson's endless sermon, she stole a few surreptitious glances at Travis from be-

neath her lashes. She could almost see the wheels
working at top speed inside his head. She was almost positive he was contemplating a hurried trip to
the airport to catch the next flight out of town and
didn't know whether she felt more like laughing or
crying. By the restless movement of his fingers, the
constant readjustment of his shoulders against the
back of the pew, it was woefully apparent to her that
he couldn't wait to leave, that his intentions had
never been honorable. Hadn't she known that all
along?

In the past Melissa had enjoyed every minute of
Sunday service. She loved to sing the beautiful old
hymns, find solace in communal prayer, worship
beside her neighbors. Today, when the old reed organ began the recessional, she was relieved that the
service was over. Tonight she promised herself to
pray for forgiveness, but right now she needed to
hustle Travis out of the church before they were
inundated with questions from a passel of well-
meaning friends.

"Kenny's case is in the car," she said as she stood
up from the pew, pushing her hand against Travis's
arm to urge him out into the aisle. "Shall we go?"

"That was a beautiful service, Lissa, and this is a
lovely old church." Travis let her step in front of
him as they proceeded toward the rear doors. "I remember it from the summer I was here. I really liked
this place."

For a man in a hurry, he certainly took his time
getting down the aisle. As they slowly passed by the
back pews, Travis politely allowed three if not four
elderly ladies to step out in front of them. His hand

on her shoulder was not being used to urge her forward but rather to pull her back so someone else could get in line. She gave him a beseeching look, but he didn't get the message.

"Isn't that Hugo Kratchett?" He nodded toward a thin white-haired man who was slowly making his way out of church with the aid of a hand-carved cane. "I thought he'd be long dead by now. Does Gus still play checkers with that old cheat?"

"Every third Wednesday night of the month," Melissa muttered balefully. "Travis, don't you think we should try to move a little faster? I saw my folks take Kenny out the side door. We can go directly to the car. Know what I mean?" She used her eyes to amplify the words and cocked her head toward the door.

She thought him particularly dense when he shrugged his answer. "We'll get there soon enough." His sentimental smile showed he had completely forgotten the reason for their haste as he lost himself in a haze of fond memories. "It's been years since I've even thought about those hilarious checker games. Every once in a while, Hugo would let me sit in for Gus. I'd really like to stop and say hello to him. Tell him I've learned a few things since he showed me how to play."

Before she could stop him, he'd put that plan into action and they were making small talk with Hugo. As Melissa had feared, when they finally made it outside, there was a group of people waiting to greet them at the bottom of the church steps. She felt like a celebrity about to be confronted by the clamoring press.

"What did I tell you?" she breathed in annoyance. Her fingers dug into Travis's arm. "Now we're in for it, and it's your own fault."

She was certain he had completely lost his mind when he tucked her arm through his and gave her a reassuring pat on the hand. "After meeting your mother, anyone else should be child's play."

"You don't understand . . . ."

He didn't wait to hear the rest of her sentence but gave her a brilliant smile, propelling them both down the stairs and into the fray. She had to admit when they were finally able to make it back to the car that Travis had been master of evasion. He had parried the questions of even the most curious matron with aplomb, giving the impression that the relationship between Melissa and himself was strictly platonic. He was Gus's nephew and since Gus wasn't feeling well this morning, Melissa had kindly offered to take him along with her to church.

"I was impressed," she admitted as she opened the trunk for Kenny's suitcase. "At next week's meeting of the ladies' circle, they'll all be talking about the dashing young man who graced them with a visit to church on Sunday."

Taking on a high-pitched nasal tone, she mimicked Eloise Baker, the reigning society matriarch of the community. "Too bad Melissa is such a small-town girl. Of course, we were all hoping she'd found a new man, but in vain—she just wouldn't suit him. He's a world traveler, you know, and she's such a homebody. Poor girl would have nothing to offer a sophisticated man like that."

Melissa thoroughly enjoyed contemplating such a

conversation, but Travis brought an end to her pleasure with his own rendition of Mrs. Baker's knowing tone. "Of course. I did hear that he was invited
to her parents' for Sunday dinner. If she's taking
him to meet the family, it might be serious. One
never knows. Maybe she's got more to offer than we
think. Perhaps she's convinced him to settle down,
that he needs a good woman and a place to call
home."

"What?" Melissa was asking for a far different explanation than the one she received. "I never invited
you to my parents' for dinner. The plan was to hand
over this suitcase, then go back home."

"Out of the question," Travis negated evenly. He
removed Melissa's suddenly lifeless hands from
Kenny's suitcase and closed the trunk himself. He
pointed to the vacant space where her parents' car
had been parked. "We'll have to deliver the suitcase,
since they've already left. Your folks are expecting us
to follow them home and join them for dinner. I
don't want to miss one bite of your mother's roast
beef, so let's get going."

"You're kidding?"

"Nope." His laughing eyes mocked her stunned
expression. "How else do you think I escaped? I
agreed that we'd both come to the house. Your mom
will be able to soften me up with a home-cooked
meal, then interrogate me over dessert."

Melissa was far too upset to say anything when he
assisted her into the passenger seat, then walked
around and got in behind the wheel. "She tempted
me with lemon-meringue pie, my favorite. The
woman is a shrewd operator all right. Found out my

weakness and took full advantage. I tried to resist, but the flesh is weak."

He hung his head, the picture of abject contrition, and Melissa couldn't help it. She burst out laughing. "You, sir, are a real glutton for punishment," she exclaimed between giggles, then quickly regained her composure as she pondered how her family might misconstrue the situation.

"I hope you know what you're doing, Travis. You're laughing this whole thing off but this is getting serious. My mother is the most famous matchmaker in the county. If word of this gets out, that speech you made up for Eloise won't be too far off the mark. Then people will really start thinking that there's something going on between us."

"Give me the keys, Lissa," he ordered gruffly, and she complied. She was in no condition to drive, and the new biting edge to his voice threw her completely. She felt like the helpless branch of a willow being buffeted this way and that by a sudden violent blast of wind. Facing down her exuberant family was one thing, but facing down an angry Travis was an entirely different matter. The gold in his eyes no longer shone with warmth but had turned hard and cold.

Travis asked for directions and she gave them in a very small voice, intimidated by the hard set of his jaw, the white-knuckled grip he'd taken on the steering wheel. The silence between them grew increasingly ominous until Travis turned down the county road that would take them to her parents' farm.

Then, without looking at her, he made a harsh

pronouncement. "Something *is* going on between us, Lissa. We both know it and it *is* serious, very serious. I want you, and I know you want me. Until we decide what we're going to do about that, I'm not leaving, no matter what other people say or think. You're going to have to stop running away from me."

He turned his head to look at her, his gaze frighteningly intent. "For both our sakes, I hope you don't wait too long. If we're not careful, we could end up doing something we'll both regret for a very long time. Think about it."

"I have thought about it," she defended, stung by his unexpected attack. "There'll be nothing to regret. I'm not getting involved with a man like you. From a few things Gus has said along the line, it sounds to me like you've got a woman in every port. I have no intention of joining that kind of sorority."

"Is that what you're afraid of?" he asked, impatiently sweeping the hair off his forehead. "Or is there some other man in your life?"

"There's *no* other man in my life," she blazed back at him.

"Not even a ghost?"

"Don't be ridiculous," she scoffed.

"Good." His voice softened, and he gave her a meaningful laugh. "Then I've got a clear field."

His arrogant remark rendered Melissa speechless for the rest of the trip to her parents' farm.

7

SEATED AT THE HEAD OF THE LONG MAHOGANY TABLE, Kenneth Kvam called for quiet, then reached for Melissa's hand. She in turn took hold of her eldest brother Burt's fingers, and the procedure was repeated around the table until everyone had joined hands. Travis was the only member of the gathering who didn't bow his head and close his eyes when the patriarch of the family began saying grace.

Instead he took advantage of the opportunity to look around the old-fashioned dining room, taking note of all the things that conveyed the history of this family. One wall was composed of built-in bookshelves, and on the middle shelf there were pictures of the Kvams with their children and grandchildren. On another, he perused what he supposed were the more distant relatives, grandparents, uncles, aunts and cousins. Yet another contained trophies, ribbons and plaques, not important awards but the minor triumphs of an average family.

Melissa, he saw, had won several 4-H blue ribbons for raising and showing stock, cooking and sewing. Her brothers boasted similar success with animals and with football and track. Kenneth Kvam was a bowler, his wife a horticulturist. There was a place set aside for each member's accomplishments, right down to the four bronzed baby shoes that were lined up on the bottom shelf.

"We give thanks Father..." Kenneth prayed, but to Travis the heartfelt words weren't nearly as meaningful as the current of love and affection he felt coursing through his fingers. He'd never experienced anything like it, couldn't recall a time when he'd grasped hold of another man's hand in fellowship and communion. It was a good feeling, very good. He closed his eyes and silently added his thanks to that being offered by Melissa's father.

"Let me help you with that, Kenny." Elaine stood up from the table a moment after the prayer was completed. "That bowl is much too hot for you boys to pick up. Melissa, will you pass the potatoes to your father? Sandy, I left the rolls in the kitchen. Will you get them for me, dear? Try the sweet potatoes, Burt. I made them just the way you like."

Suppressing his grin, Travis watched as the Kvam siblings quickly carried out their orders. Kenny and Burt's two young sons, Teddy and Jerry waited patiently for their grandmother to spoon some creamed carrots onto their plates. Melissa passed her father the potatoes. Burt's wife, Sandy, left the table to search out the forgotten rolls, while Burt helped himself to a huge helping of sweet potatoes. Since Travis had never been fond of sweet potatoes, he didn't take any when Burt handed him the bowl.

"You still look a bit peaked to me, Travis." Elaine intercepted the bowl before he could pass it on and plopped it back into his hands. "You should eat lots of vegetables. They're chock full of vitamins."

Travis found he was as quick as the others to follow the dictates of the petite blond woman in charge. He glanced at Melissa from beneath his lashes as he reluctantly placed a small portion of the sweet orange potatoes on his plate. To his surprise, he found that Melissa wasn't the only one who was sympathizing with him. Burt leaned over and whispered conspiratorially in his ear. "If you eat here often enough, you'll develop a taste for them. It's your only choice."

To prevent his wife from overhearing Burt's comments, Kenneth winked at Travis, then stated in a louder than normal tone, "I wish you'd sit down, mother. The rest of us don't feel comfortable eating while you're hovering about like that. Bad for the digestion."

"In a minute, dear," Elaine agreed, smiling happily as the last of the dishes made their rounds of the table. "I just want to make sure everyone has what they need. Eat everything on your plates, boys." She patted each of her grandsons on the head as she made her way back to her seat next to Travis. "Then grandpa will get you a treat at the zoo. Won't you, Kenneth?"

When Elaine asked Travis if he were enjoying the sweet potatoes and he said they were fine, he felt as if he were part of an affectionate conspiracy that had probably been in operation for years. For the remainder of the meal, he followed everyone else's lead as they sought to appease Elaine without gaining two hundred pounds. He got away with only two helpings of roast beef and mashed potatoes and couldn't prevent his gloating expression when Melissa couldn't talk herself out of a third helping of carrots. He didn't think he'd ever enjoyed a meal more and said so over dessert.

"Why, thank you, Travis." Elaine smiled as she lowered a second huge piece of lemon meringue pie onto his plate. "At least someone here appreciates my cooking."

"You know I'm on a diet, Mother Kvam," Sandy reminded as she poured the adults some coffee. "Teddy's four years old, and I still haven't lost the weight I put on when I was pregnant."

"I ate too many sweet potatoes." Burt grinned at his wife who was as slender today as the day they'd gotten married. "Don't have room for another bite."

Kenneth offered the excuse that his stomach was slightly upset, and Melissa changed the subject. "I'll start clearing the table so dad and the boys can be on their way to the zoo. Kenny's been looking forward to this for weeks." She glared at her son, daring him to say different, but the boy had learned quite a lot about his grandmother in his five short years.

"Can we be excused now, grandma? We've gotta get going."

Elaine was effectively mollified by the prospect of organizing her husband and grandsons for their up-coming excursion. Taking Kenny and Teddy by the hand, she followed Melissa out of the dining room, calling over her shoulder, "Come along, Jerry. Hurry up now, father. You heard your grandson. Find sweaters for your boys, Burt, and we'll meet you at the car."

Moments later, Travis and Sandra Kvam were alone in the dining room. Slender and dark, with brown eyes and auburn hair, Sandra was the only person present, other than Travis, who wasn't a blonde. "Your two boys look a lot like their father," Travis observed, hoping to start a conversation with the first "in-law" he'd met thus far.

Sandra laughed. "Who looks a lot like his father and all the Kvams before them. There are some awfully strong genes in this family."

"Do all of them have that incredibly light hair?"

Sandra nodded. "Gary and his son and daughter are blondes too. The only one who looks a little bit different is the youngest brother, Jamie. Believe it or not, he's got red hair and freckles."

"Who does?" Melissa asked, as she reentered the room. Sinking down in the chair next to Sandy's, she promptly took a fortifying drink of her coffee.

"Jamie," Sandy said. "I was telling Travis about the rest of the family."

"If you wait a few minutes, mother will be happy to tell you more things than you'd care to know about all of us," Melissa pronounced, an edge to her voice.

It wasn't usual for her to speak like that about her mother, and Sandy called her on it. "Why do you sound so upset, Mel? You're mother's justifiably proud of her family. What's wrong with that?"

Melissa sighed. "Nothing. I just thought Travis should be prepared, that's all. She's probably going to show him all the pictures in the family album. Isn't that what she did to you the first time you came out here?"

"Have things progressed that far between you two?" Sandy asked, her dark eyes going wide with surprise.

Melissa could have gladly bitten off her own

tongue and almost did when Travis supplied the answer. "Far enough that I'd enjoy seeing that album. I'll bet you were an awfully cute baby, Lissa." His brown eyes danced gleefully as he inquired hopefully, "Any chance one of those pictures will include a blond baby girl and a bearskin rug?"

"Travis!" Melissa choked out, her cheeks the color of a red rose.

Laughing, Sandra rose from her chair. "Stay here, Mel. I'm going to start on those dishes so Burt and I can head home. We've got a whole week without the boys, and I'm going to take advantage of every second."

Melissa waited until she heard the squeaking door of the dishwasher before she cut into Travis. "What are you trying to do? Make everyone think we're—we're—?"

He filled in her blank with urbane ease. "Close friends? Lovers? Do you like the sound of either of those?"

"We're not friends or lovers."

"I didn't say we were," he corrected. "I asked if you liked the sound of them. You know which one I'd prefer. Friends is nice, but I want us to be lovers, and the sooner the better."

Melissa's hand fluttered to her breast to calm the tumultuous beating of her heart. "How can you say something like that? Right here in my parents' house!"

"What difference does it make where I say it?"

"It makes all the difference in the world." Melissa pushed back her chair, smoting him with troubled blue eyes. "This isn't the time or the place."

"Okay," he agreed, his heated gaze following every move she made as she began stacking the dishes that remained on the table. "If I pick a better time and place, will you give me the answer I want?"

"Not unless it's what I want, too." Melissa refused to look at him as she picked up the stack of dishes. She started toward the kitchen, but she heard the soft comment he made as she pushed through the swinging wooden door.

"I'll make sure you want it, sweetheart. Very sure."

"HOW TERRIBLE FOR YOU!" Elaine reached across the sofa and patted Travis's hand. "You two must have grown very close after five years of working together."

"Yes." Travis's voice was harsh. "He was a good foreman but an even better friend. I didn't realize that until after he was killed, when it was too damned late to tell him."

"We always seem to appreciate people more after they're gone." Elaine agreed softly. "I think most people have trouble telling others how they feel. I know I do. I try to show them that I care, but I hardly ever say the words."

Travis gazed thoughtfully into Elaine's kindly blue eyes. "Sometimes I think I should have died instead of Frank. I'm not close to my family but he....." Travis struggled to put his painful thoughts into words, not knowing how this amazing woman had gotten him started, but feeling as if another piece of some heavy burden was being lifted off his shoulders with every word he spoke. "He left a wife and six kids. If I had gone out to check on those girders, instead of sending Frank, he'd be home with them right now. So many people loved him, and were counting on his coming back."

"You can't feel guilty, Travis, even though that's perfectly natural," Elaine admonished gently. "When my mother died, I felt guilty because I was so busy raising my children, I didn't get over to see her that often. I was sure that if I had been there the day she suffered her stroke, she wouldn't have died. I was afraid she passed on without knowing how much I cared."

Travis managed a weak smile. "That's exactly how I feel. If I had been out on that bridge, Frank wouldn't have been killed. Maybe then I would have had the chance to tell him that I considered him my best friend."

"Isn't it more likely that you'd be dead, too?"

After a long silence Travis finally choked out, "Yes. No man could have lived through that explosion. I was quite far away, and I still ended up with a concussion and a bunch of broken ribs. It's just that I feel so rotten about Frank. He was one of the few members of our crew who was married and had children. It seems so unfair."

"Only to those left behind," Elaine observed. "Death marks the end of our being able to show love to someone, but I firmly believe there's an even greater love waiting for them somewhere else. The rest of us just have to go on loving and caring for the living. It's all we can do."

"Bless you, mom," Melissa mouthed silently as

she listened to her mother's soothing words of wisdom, regretting all the uncomplimentary thoughts she'd had about her today. How many times had she sensed that Travis had suffered a far greater hurt in the explosion than he'd let on? By his lightened expression, she could tell that her mother had helped him to accept something that had never been his fault. She was experiencing the same kind of acceptance herself.

Like Travis, she'd never spoken to anyone about the guilt she felt at Gordy's death, letting the past discolor the future. Her mother's words were like a balm, soothing away the hurtful memories, easing the pain of helplessness. Never again would she think that if she'd been all Gordy needed, he wouldn't have died. All she could do was go on, loving and caring for the living.

For the first time, she allowed herself to consider the possibility that Travis might really feel something for her. He wanted them to become lovers, but perhaps he wanted even more. Was he seeing himself with a wife and child? A place to call home, as he'd joked about earlier? Was he picturing a future with her? The description he'd given her mother about himself and his life-style sounded so lonely.

Sometimes she got the feeling that, with the exception of Gus, he'd never been close to anyone, that he had always been alone. It sounded as if he rarely saw his parents—often the case with adult children. They left home and slowly stretched their family bonds until they were so thin, the slightest strain could break them.

Whatever had caused Travis's bitterness toward

his parents didn't really matter, but she sensed that he had very little affection for them. She didn't know what it would be like to be totally estranged from her family. She couldn't imagine the loneliness of having no one to turn to in times of trouble. She could always count on her parents, her brothers and their wives, and Gus and Kenny. Who did Travis have? What caused that terrible hunger she sometimes saw in his eyes when he looked at her or her son? Was it loneliness? Was that what attracted her to him?

She knew all about loneliness, and her heart swelled with empathy. Maybe it wouldn't be so wrong for them to turn to each other, alleviate that desolate void they both lived with. It wouldn't be so terrible to give in to the aching need she had to be held in a strong man's arms—Travis's strong arms.

AFTER HE'D DRIVEN THEM A FEW MILES down the road, Travis glanced at Melissa. "You're mother's quite a woman," he asserted stoutly, trying to draw her attention away from the side window where it had been fixed ever since they'd gotten back into her car. "I think you're too hard on her. She loves you very much."

As he had hoped, Melissa turned to look at him. He couldn't have been more surprised by her sweet smile. "I know she does," she vowed brightly. "Sometimes I lose sight of that fact, but then she goes and does something so nice, I can't deny it. I love her, too."

"My, my," Travis drawled, switching his gaze back to the road as he negotiated a sharp curve.

"That's quite a change of tune since this morning. Did she do something particularly nice this afternoon that I didn't notice? Other than plying us with so much food I feared I'd never get off the couch?"

"She let you sleep it off," Melissa reminded pointedly, unwilling to relate the real reason for her "change in tune." She didn't think he'd appreciate her knowing that she'd overheard his conversation with her mother.

With a mischievous twinkle in her blue eyes, she glanced at her watch. "For over an hour. I thought that was very kind of her."

A pink tinge crept along Travis's jaw. "I can't believe I did that. One minute I was listening to you two talking out in the kitchen and the next, I was asleep on the couch."

"Perhaps you needed the rest," she suggested gently.

He cast her a sharp, questioning gaze, but nodded. "I haven't been sleeping very well lately. Must be the quiet. I'm not used to it."

"Maybe so." She was willing to accept any excuse he cared to make. Men were so strange. They hated showing the slightest sign of vulnerability, yet it was that trait that made them so endearing. How could a woman feel needed if her man never showed the slightest sign of any weakness? Never required more from her than the use of her body?

At the moment, Travis looked like a man who'd just been confronted with the boy inside himself, the defenseless child he'd spent years suppressing. "When I woke up, you and your mother were just sitting there staring at me. Might I ask what you found so fascinating?"

She pretended to give his question careful consideration, then replied in a serious tone, "You're awfully cute when you're asleep, Travis."

His jaw dropped open with shock, and the pink tinge became a full-scale flush. She laughed in delight.

"Women!" he mumbled under his breath, then tried to distract her apparent fascination with his reddened cheeks by accusing, "One of you stole my shoes."

"I did." She chuckled, thoroughly enjoying his discomfort. "One of the first rules mother taught us was never to put our shoes on the furniture. I also put that pillow under your head. Otherwise, you'd now be suffering from a very stiff neck."

"Why didn't you try waking me up instead of making me more comfortable?" He kept his eyes fixed on the road as they topped a hill. "It might have been less embarrassing."

"You're admitting that you were embarrassed?"

"You don't have to look so pleased about it." Travis's grin told her that her complacency really didn't bother him at all. "What have I ever done to you?"

"Want a list?" Her corresponding smile was equally lighthearted.

The remainder of the drive back to Wintersfield was filled with teasing banter, the kind of flirtatious remarks that skirted deeper implications neither of them was ready to confront. When they arrived at the farm, parked the car and walked side by side into the house, it seemed perfectly natural, seemed right.

"How do you feel about grilled cheese sandwiches for supper?" Melissa asked as she walked ahead of Travis into the kitchen.

Travis groaned. "I was thinking along the lines of a single stalk of celery."

"Seriously?"

"No. Sandwiches are fine." Travis looked down at his flat stomach. "I'm surprised your father doesn't weigh a thousand pounds if your mother cooks like that every day."

"She does." Melissa opened the bread box. "It's a good thing dad has work to do that keeps the weight off. That's one good thing about being a farmer. You can eat a lot, then go do chores so you'll have room for more." A frown of regret furrowed her brow. "Speaking of chores, after we eat, I'll have to get out to the barn and do the milking."

"I'll help," Travis said as he took off his suit coat and hung it over a kitchen chair. He sat down at the table. "It shouldn't take too long with both of us doing it."

Melissa was about to open the refrigerator when she saw the piece of white paper taped to the door. "What a darling!"

"I'll help every day if you keep calling me darling," Travis confided suggestively, loosening his tie. He draped it over his coat.

"Not you." She dashed his hopes. "Gus is the darling. He's gone and done the milking for me and is eating supper with Hugo. He must be feeling better, or he'd never attempt a hot game of checkers on an off night." She went to the south window and pulled back the chintz curtain. "It looks like he went out and started early. The lights are already off in the milk house."

"Good man," Travis declared enthusiastically. "For that, I'll stop being hurt that I'm not the darling you had in mind. He's given me the chance to earn the term by a far more enjoyable means."

Melissa decided to take that remark in her stride. Travis was very adept with the innuendos, but she was fast learning how to cope with them. "Terrific. You can start by helping me make supper. I'll do the sandwiches, and you can make the salad...darling."

The provocative teasing continued all through supper but ended soon after, replaced by an uncomfortable tension. They were completely alone with nothing to stop them from culminating their desire for each other except Melissa's inhibitions. What was she supposed to do now? Ignore the moral code of a lifetime and succumb to the overwhelming desire that crackled between them? If she made love to him, it would mean more to her than giving in to physical attraction. Did Travis feel the same way?

She wanted him, but still hadn't worked out the conflicts in her mind. She knew he needed her, was searching for solace, trying to alleviate his loneliness. No matter how much she feared being nothing more to him than that, she needed the same things from him. Even so, if she decided to risk giving herself to a man who might want nothing else but her body, how would she go about it? Invite him up to her bedroom? Take off her clothes and entice him into her arms?

Since she wasn't the seductive type, she knew she'd never do that. Travis would have to take the first step, make the decision for her. She suggested they adjourn to the living room to watch a television program and was greatly disappointed by his immediate compliance.

"Great!" he enthused.

Her shoulders sagged in defeat as she followed his retreating back into the other room. When she arrived in the living room, he was already making himself comfortable on the couch. So much for her seductive powers.

After adjusting the portable antenna to get the best reception, Melissa stared for a few moments at the screen. Then, satisfied that the picture wouldn't begin to roll, she backed to the couch. But when she sat down, the large cushion had a far different texture than the one she'd expected. "Travis!"

"Too late, my lovely Lissa," Travis growled throatily as he swiftly adjusted her legs across his lap, then pushed down on her shoulder until her head was resting in the crook of his arm. His eyes lingered on the tantalizing curve of her lips. "It's hell to want a woman as badly as I want you, and I'm going to do something about it right now."

She felt the tension in him as she lifted her startled eyes to his face. She now saw what only seconds ago had been concealed by his thick mahogany lashes. It was naked hunger—so intense she was frightened. She had wanted him to take the first step, but now that he had, what if she disappointed him? She'd never been with any man but Gordy, wasn't half as experienced as Travis might expect. There was nothing sophisticated about her, and she still wasn't sure she could handle a physical relationship with Travis when he offered no commitment. "I'm not sure..." she whispered uncertainly.

The lights went on in his eyes, an intense gold blaze, brighter than ever. "You'll be sure, Lissa," he promised, lowering his lips to the corner of her mouth. "As sure as I am."

Melissa's lips parted to voice her insecurity, but he sealed the words in her throat. With one hand in her hair, he held her head in place, his tongue thrusting deeply into her mouth, proving his certainty with an exploration that left no room for doubt.

Beneath the impact of his mouth, Melissa trembled, feeling as if he was inexorably staking a claim that would be impossible to revoke. His fingers were snarled in her hair, threading and twisting the strands as if they were slender gold chains that bound her to him. His tongue imparted a heavy drug that dulled every sense save one—need. She needed him just as badly as he needed her, and neither of them could put if off any longer.

"Seeing you in that skirt has been driving me crazy all day," he muttered, placing moist kisses along the line of her cheek to her ear. "Every time you'd move those exquisite, long legs of yours, I'd have visions of swiss lace running under my fingers." One hand rode up beneath her floral-print skirt, seeking the outer curve of her calf, her thigh, then her hip. "Just like this." He drew a ragged, gasping breath.

She shivered with waiting tension, hypnotized by his soft velvet voice, the caressing fervor of his lips, the trembling wonder in his searching hands. She felt weak, far too weak to do anything but go with

him when he slid off the cushions to the floor. As if
he was making a bed for her, he reached for the satin
throw pillow in the corner of the couch. With one
hand he lifted her head and slid the pillow beneath
it with the other. Lovingly he adjusted her hips on
the thick pile of the blue shag rug, his eyes gleaming
with a possessive fire.

Getting back to his feet, he began removing his
gold cuff links, then unbuttoned his shirt. His
fingers fumbled slightly, indicating his inner agitation. If she wanted him to stop, now was the time to
tell him, but her throat was too dry to form words.
When he drew off his shirt and flung it away from
him, she couldn't prevent a tiny gasp. The rib belt
was gone, the dark bruise fading.

Her eyes collided with the massive muscles of his
shoulders and chest, gleaming in the white light
from the television before he leaned over and turned
the set off. The only illumination left in the room
came from the setting sun, a soft golden haze that
shimmered across his tanned skin, gilding the light
streaks in his rich brown hair.

He trembled as her glowing eyes swept over his
body and smiled gently at her when he reached for
the gold buckle on his thin leather belt. When her
fingers traveled to her blouse, he shook his head.
"Let me, Lissa. I want to undress you myself."

He made short work of taking off his shoes and
socks, then stripped off his pants and briefs before
kneeling down beside her. "I'm shaking like a boy
on his first date. That's how you make me feel."

"You're no boy, Travis," she murmured throatily,
unable to take her eyes off his body, admiring the

contrasting texture of curling dark hair and smooth bronze flesh.

His surging arousal left her in no doubt about what he was feeling. She was appalled by his blunt honesty but even more excited. No man had ever made her feel this way, so beautiful, so desirable that he feared losing control. She had trouble swallowing, breathing. He was beautiful, so beautiful, and she lifted her hand to touch him.

"Not yet," he pleaded roughly. "When I feel your hands on me, I want you to be naked, too. Otherwise—"

She was half afraid she might die before he completed undressing her. It was a slow, tortuous process that began with her shoes. First one flimsy sling-back, then the other was carefully removed. After which, he massaged her feet with strong fingers, easing the tension in each instep, then making her toes curl as his fingers trailed up her legs.

He drew the thin fabric of her skirt down, pulling the elastic waist over her hips, then slowly lower until he could lift it away from her ankles. He grew impatient by the time he'd unbuttoned her blouse, and she was elated when he finally slipped his knee beneath her shoulders and dragged the garment off.

She closed her eyes when she felt his fingers on the clasp of her bra, then drawing it away from her breasts. She kept her eyes closed as he inserted his thumbs in the sheer panty of her hose, then peeled them down. She was naked except for her white panties and then even those were stripped away. Opening her eyes she looked into the flaming hunger in his as he surveyed her nakedness.

"No man should need a woman this badly." His voice was shaking. He cleared his throat as he reached out with one finger and touched the pointed nipple of her full breast. "You're a very dangerous lady, Melissa Lindstrand. I'm playing with fire, and I don't even care that I'm about to get third-degree burns."

Those were the last words he spoke before grasping her arms and pulling her naked body against his. It was an eclectic fusion, the hardness of man and the softness of woman, combining their textures and forms, yearning to be one. Travis didn't allow that to happen, however, until he'd discovered every difference between his body and hers.

In a world of incoherent thought, wondrous feeling, Melissa was lost, aware of nothing but the power Travis generated, the magic he performed on her oversensitized flesh. Her body responded on the most primitive of levels, writhing and twisting beneath him as he provoked a series of surrenders with his mouth, his hands and the intimate probings of his tongue. He used his strength to gently trap her, then released her so she could use her own to entrap him.

Together they searched for and found the sources of their greatest pleasure, kissing and stroking each new discovery with intoxicated frenzy. Travis found that she could barely stand the feel of his mouth on the undersides of her breasts. Melissa learned that Travis couldn't take her kisses on the taut flesh stretched over his hips.

By the time they reached the last plateau, the highest level of sensation, they were both quivering uncontrollably. Melissa had never felt such joy. Relying on instinct to see her through what she'd never known before, she used the elemental power she had to make him groan, to bring his body to life in a way that thrilled her to the deepest part of her being. He had the same power, and when he finally spread her thighs apart with one knee and thrust himself inside her, she wrapped her legs tightly around his hips.

He surged forward with slow measures of male force and exquisite heat. When at last he was fully buried, he began moving his hips, establishing the rhythm of a male possessing his woman. Melissa knew with her heart and her mind that this was right and good, was as sure as he had been that this was the ultimate danger, but she had no fear. She was with Travis and he with her as they clung to each other and became one.

For a long time, neither of them moved. They waited until the last ragged breath had calmed, the last shiver rippled away. Melissa lay peacefully in the damp tangle of arms and legs, unwilling to break contact. She could feel her lashes against Travis's chest, the involuntary contraction of his skin when she blinked. Even now it seemed, when he was replete with lovemaking, her slightest touch brought an instant response. It was heady knowledge. She wanted more information.

He was like a sleepy lion, but the feel of her tongue on his chest brought him out of his somnolent state. "You're a cruel little tease, Lissa," he complained, his voice husky with satisfaction.

"No one's ever called me little." Melissa giggled,

tracing the pattern of curling chest hair with an inquisitive finger until a large hand came down over it, keeping it still.

"Maybe I think of you as little because you've made me feel like one hell of a man. People tell me I already have an outsized ego, but I've never felt this good about myself."

"I feel pretty good myself," Melissa mused, astonished that it was the truth. She felt wonderful, more of a woman than ever before in her life. She could make a man tremble!

He spoke her thoughts out loud at almost the same time. "Do you have any idea what it does to man when he can make a woman tremble with wanting him? My God, Lissa. That was—incredible."

"Mmm," she agreed happily, and snuggled down on his chest. Moments later, she was asleep. She didn't stir when Travis lifted her away from him. She didn't hear him when he got dressed. Nor was she aware when he stood staring at her sleeping form, curled up like a baby on the rug.

Travis glanced at the stairs, considered carrying her to her bedroom, then decided against it. Here in this room she was all his, but upstairs there were bound to be reminders of another man, other claims that tied her to the past. He wanted no reminders, and he didn't want her to feel the slightest guilt. He found a comforter folded over the back of a rocking chair and tenderly covered her with it. *Don't regret this in the morning, Lissa,* he pleaded silently. *Please don't regret this.*

He went down on one knee and placed a soft kiss

on her cheek. "There's no going back, Lissa," he whispered. "After this, there's no going back for either of us."

8

A DISTANT HORN sang a hymn of nature. A rush of wind blew against her face as the festive sounds of peasant merrymaking filled the fertile meadowland. The gaily colored ribbons streaming from her bridal crown of flowers mingled with her hair as she tilted her face upward and smiled at her new husband.

The barn door slammed shut, the clatter of the wood against the frame shattering the lilting music of Smetana, and Melissa was no longer one of the dancers stepping lightly across the lush flower-strewed meadow depicted so beautifully in *From Bohemia's Meadows and Forests*. She wasn't wearing a richly embroidered velvet vest, nor were frothy layers of lace-trimmed petticoats swirling around her. Heavy mud-spattered boots covered her feet. One lone, rather bedraggled ribbon held her hair away from her face, and baggy overalls flapped against her slender legs as she moved between the cows.

"I didn't expect to see you this early," she said, smiling weakly at the man whose entrance had shattered her fantasy and reminded her of an equally romantic but painful reality. She and Travis had become lovers last night, but she was probably fooling herself if she thought they would ever be more.

He might be the groom in her woodland fantasy, but that had only been part of a pleasant daydream. In reality, she had given him what he'd wanted and now, even though she'd foolishly fallen in love with him, there was nothing to prevent him from moving on.

"When in Rome...." Travis's eyes twinkled with those golden highlights that continually entranced her, and his lips spread into a maddening grin. "I thought I'd lend you a hand, as well as learn a little more about this operation."

"Why should you want to learn?" she probed curiously, hoping he would tell her what she really wanted to hear—that he'd fallen in love with her too and would stay on at Wintersfield.

Avoiding his eyes, she transferred the milk from the receiving pan to the conveyer in the middle of the aisle. When she got no answer to her question, she pressed, "Milking cows and plowing fields doesn't strike me as the kind of thing an international engineer would find too interesting." She continued working, trying not to break her rhythm as she talked with Travis.

"We engineers never know what kind of situation we might encounter," was his smooth reply. "I like to be prepared."

Smetana's lyrical music swelled around her, but Melissa could no longer hear the beautiful tone poem painting a sunlit picture of an Austrian pastoral wedding. Every one of her senses was tuned to this man, whose hair and eyes had captured all the sunlight. His presence made her feel as firmly confined as if she'd been one of the cows held in place by a heavy stanchion snapped around her neck. But he was free—free to pick up and go at any time.

"And are you always prepared?" she asked, removing another milking machine and dumping the contents into the conveyer.

"Not always. Sometimes there are some surprises I hadn't counted on."

Melissa kept her eyes directed on her work, her hands mechanically performing each task without really getting signals from her brain. Is that what she was? A surprise he hadn't counted on?

"What do you do when you encounter these surprises, as you call them?" She purposely busied herself, afraid of his answer.

Fiddling with the compressor, she kept herself occupied, kept herself from drinking in his every detail. How could he look so good this early in the morning?

"I readjust my thinking, come up with a new plan and try to work out all the details to everyone's satisfaction."

"Oh." She wondered what part of his new plan, if any, included her but didn't dare ask.

"I knew it," he sighed. "I knew you'd act like this today."

"Like what?" she inquired.

"Like you regret what happened last night. Now that you've had time to think, you're afraid of what the neighbors might say, aren't you?"

"That might not be important to you, but you haven't lived here all your life."

Travis ran one hand through his hair in exasperation. "Dammit, Lissa, I don't give a hang what anyone thinks but you. What we shared was beautiful, and I'm not going to let you ruin it with regrets.''

Seeing the hurt in his eyes, she explained, ''I don't regret it, but we hardly know each other, Travis. Maybe we turned to each other out of loneliness. I . . . I haven't been with a man since Gordy. I don't know if you're involved with a woman somewhere, but because of your accident, you probably haven't—''

''I'm not involved with a woman somewhere,'' he interrupted. ''What kind of man do you think I am?''

''That's just it, Travis,'' she said with a quiet emphasis. ''I don't know what kind of man you are, but I do know me. I'm not the kind of woman who can have a casual affair.''

''I hate to bring this up, Lissa, but you're already having one.'' Seeing her stricken expression, he relented, ''Don't look like that. What's happening between us is anything but casual.''

''We don't know enough about each other to tell if it's serious or not.''

''All right then, let's take some time to get to know each other—starting today.''

Her eyes searched his. Reading nothing but sincerity in his steady gaze, she murmured softly, ''I think that might be a good idea, but I want to set some ground rules first.''

She had only intended to insist that they be discreet, but he didn't give her the chance. An angry explosion went off in his eyes. ''I make my own rules, Melissa, especially with women.'' His tone was full of masculine superiority.

"Not with this woman," she insisted, moving for security behind a huge Holstein.

"Oh?" He took a threatening step toward her, his dark eyes gleaming with challenge. "Why don't you come out from behind that cow," he suggested silkily.

"Why?"

"Because we're going to get something straight before your morals get in the way again. Come out here."

"I'm not going anywhere!" she shot back with bravado.

Too late she realized he was a man who shouldn't be challenged. Every taut muscle in his body relayed that message to her.

"Then I'll come to you," he stated with deceptive calm.

He nudged the cow aside with his hip and sidled into the station. A split second later she was lifted off her feet and flung over his shoulder.

"Put me down!" she ordered, trying to retain some dignity. "You're not a caveman."

He chuckled. "No, I'm not. A caveman would have grabbed you by the hair."

He strode briskly down the center aisle until he reached the far end of the barn, where he unceremoniously tossed her onto a pile of loose hay. Then, he flung himself on top of her, restraining her indignant body beneath his. With one hand, he trapped her face and held it still.

"Rule number one. As long as I'm here, this is the way we'll start the day," his low voice proclaimed just before his mouth came down on hers.

His kiss was thorough, demanding her response, branding her with the seal of his lips. When she could no longer deny his ownership, she responded.

Her arms came up around his back, her nails digging convulsively into the material of his shirt. He went on kissing her until she was limp, and when he finally lifted his head, she barely remembered where they were.

"Would you like to hear rule number two?" he drawled.

"Uh-uh," she negated, fearing she didn't have the strength to take any more.

"You're going to hear it anyway." His smile was a mixture of delight and boyish mischief. With one hand, he hauled her to her feet. "The rule is, we greet each other pleasantly. I'll start." The caressing inflection in his tone was as potent as his kiss. "Good morning, Lissa."

"Good morning, Travis," she obeyed willingly, then stiffened with a sudden realization. "The milking machines!"

She ran down the aisle and swiftly turned off the machine in the first station. After removing it from the cow, she started lugging the pan to the aisle. Travis moved forward and took it out of her hands. "Let me carry this."

"But you can't...I mean...isn't it too heavy?" What a dumb question! If he could lift her, he could easily lift a pan of milk.

His answer was a wide, knowing grin, one that dazzled and sought to remind her of their recent kiss. "For some reason, I'm feeling very fit this morning." He tilted the pan and started emptying it.

"I told you I was a fast healer," he said as he carried the pan to the waiting milk machine. "Show me how this thing goes back on and then what to do next."

She showed him that and a lot of other things about the farm during the rest of that day. He was an eager and quick pupil, especially with the large machinery. The tractors were no problem, as they operated exactly like the bulldozers he was familiar with. All Melissa really had to explain was the purpose and operation of the many attachments that were coupled to the tractor.

It had been obvious from the first that Travis hadn't acquired his deep tan, well-toned muscles and calloused hands by spending all his time behind a drawing board. There was too much energy sheathed in his hard body for him to merely plan and direct a project. Instead, he totally immersed himself in it, experiencing every facet with the same fervor with which he made love.

He wasn't content to simply learn about the farm, he had to *do* the work. Since the sun had finally decided to shine, the ground was dry enough to cut the alfalfa, and Travis volunteered to do it. For the rest of the day, Melissa found herself with time on her hands. Kenny was gone for the week, and Travis had taken her place in the field. It was a luxury to be able to do the accounts in the middle of the day, actually give the house a good cleaning, tend the vegetable garden and prepare Travis something special for supper. It was nice to be able to turn the field-work over to somebody else for a change.

"With a little more practice you'll probably make

a lemon pie almost as good as your mother's," Travis commented that night as he patted his full stomach.

"Well, thank you very much," Melissa sniffed in mock annoyance. She rose from the table and started to clear, eyeing the half-empty pie plate with a raised brow. "Since I only had one piece and neither Gus nor Kenny are here, I'd say you're to be commended for downing two pieces of this miserable pie."

"I accept your award for service above and beyond the call of duty," Travis returned her banter with a twinkling grin, then sobered. "Come here," he growled.

There was no mistaking the intention in his smoldering gaze, but Melissa had already succumbed to two of his orders today and that was enough. She didn't want him to think he was going to have everything his own way. He might have won the first skirmish, but the war wasn't over yet.

"Here." She picked up a dish towel and tossed it at him. "I'll wash. You dry. Rule three. When you eat my food, you help with the dishes."

"You're a hard woman, Lissa, mighty hard," he chided playfully.

Coming up out of his chair, Travis studied the dish towel he held in his hands. "First you make me get up at the crack of dawn, slave all day under a hot sun, then expect me to do the dishes." Taking a corner of the towel in each hand, he twirled it into a rope as he slowly sauntered across the kitchen floor.

Melissa's hands paused in their scrubbing of a frying pan. "You'd better not be planning to hit me with that or you've had the last piece of my lemon meringue you're ever going to get." She whirled around to defend herself, but instead of flicking the towel at her, he neatly flipped it over her head and tugged her into his arms.

"Gotcha!" He grinned down at her. "Mmm, first lemon pie and now lemon-scented soap. All those lemons ought to make you pucker real good." His mouth covered hers before she could escape.

Perversely, she kept her lips tightly closed.

"Lissa, you're not giving me my reward," Travis murmured.

"You don't deserve one," she teased.

As soon as the last word left her throat, his mouth covered hers again and his tongue slid past her relaxed guard. He swept through her mouth, conquered it, then challenged her to a duel. It was one she couldn't resist as his hands strayed along her spine, down into the small of her back. The dish towel fell silently to the floor, and his fingertips slipped beneath her pullover to skim along her bare skin.

The playful parrying and riposting subtly changed to feather-light strokes that fanned the embers of desire Melissa had tried hard to extinguish all day. They burst into full flame as Travis's heaving chest made contact with the fullness of her breasts. That she could always arouse such a reaction from him was heady stuff, and Melissa stepped into the warmth of his body, wound her arms around his neck.

"Lissa...Lissa..." he chanted as he rained kisses along her cheek and throat. "I've waited all day for this." His lips pressed moistly against the side of her neck, his rapid breath fanned warmly into her ear. The effect was so wildly tingling that she began to squirm. "God, don't do that, or I'll make love to you right here on the kitchen floor," he warned thickly.

Regretfully she stepped out of his arms and strove for a light tone, "We'd better quit lollygagging and get these dishes done. There's a herd of anxious ladies waiting beyond the barn." She turned back to the sink of sudsy water. The warm water felt cold in contrast to her heated skin as she reached beneath the surface and started wildly scrubbing at the pan.

"Lollygagging? You call it lollygagging?" he asked, incredulously.

"Yes." She giggled and thrust the pan under the tap to rinse it. "Here." She thrust the dripping pan into his hands and turned back to the sink. "Let's stop wasting time."

Travis bent down, picked up the towel off the floor and started drying the pan. "I was right, you know," he accused.

"About what?" she asked as she clattered their plates into the dishwasher.

"You *are* a hard woman. You set off an explosion in me, but instead of your gorgeous body, I get a dish towel."

"How much reward do you expect for two lousy pieces of pie?" She stopped washing and tossed him a mischievous grin.

"A lot more, my lovely Lissa, and you damned well know it," he pronounced softly. He devoured her with his eyes, then walked rapidly to the door. "I'd better go to the barn right now, or those dishes will never get done."

Twenty minutes later, when Melissa arrived in the barn, she could hear the compressors as well as the music.

"You'll have to wait just awhile longer, little girls."

It was Travis's voice, but who on earth was he talking to? Gus wasn't back from his dinner at the Kohlers'. Melissa followed the sound, startled when she saw Travis leaning over the front of the calf pen, stretching one long arm over the side. He turned toward her when he heard the sound of her boots against the barn floor.

"Hi," he greeted her, an endearing softness in both his tone and expression. When he placed an arm around her waist and pulled her closer, it seemed perfectly natural to relax against him.

"Aren't those the prettiest calves you've ever seen?" he asked, nodding toward the two black-and-white creatures vying for attention at the front of the pen. His broad hand reached in, patting one head and then the other.

Melissa giggled.

"What's so funny?" he demanded.

"You are. You sound like a proud parent showing off his progeny."

"I guess I feel that way. After all, I did help bring these two little girls into the world," he elaborated a bit defensively. "Don't you feel anything? You helped, too."

"Sure I feel something for them," Melissa confirmed evenly. "They're prime dairy stock and in another year they'll start producing. Those two are worth a lot of money."

"I think you've let that practical nature of yours warp your thinking," Travis charged brusquely. "You can't be the same softhearted woman who crooned and commiserated with the mothers all through delivery."

"That was different." Melissa pulled away and started toward the waiting milk cows, trying to hide her embarrassment at being reminded of the ways she talked to the laboring heifers that night.

"Not so fast." He captured one of her hands and yanked her back against him. Gently raising her chin with his thumb, he forced her to look straight into his eyes and ordered, "Tell me again that you can look at those cute little calves and see nothing but dollar signs."

"Okay," she admitted begrudgingly. "I do think they're cute, but there's nothing wrong with being practical. A farmer can't afford to make every animal a pet."

"I retract my earlier judgment." He moved his hand over her hip, caressing her curves. "There's nothing hard about you. You're soft and warm and...." He started to lower his head but Melissa ducked away.

"Travis," she warned, although she would have liked to stay in his arms. "Those cows won't wait patiently forever. We need to get the milking done." She spun away from him and started toward the cows.

"I know—we're lollygagging," he remarked resignedly as much to himself as to her.

The milking process was accomplished in record time, and they were just finishing cleaning the machines when Travis said, "You know I've been thinking. We ought to install an automatic feeder. I saw a computerized mechanism that mixed and measured each animal's portion according to the specifications punched in. It would sure save a lot of time. We've already got automatic watering."

"Install computers in this barn?" She shook her head wonderingly. "Do you have any idea how much that would cost?"

"Sure, but I've been working out a few facts on that. You see, if we didn't spend so much time on the feeding, we could milk more cows and increase production. I haven't worked it all out yet, but the computer should pay for itself."

"Listen, genius." Melissa flicked the light off as they left the milk house. "First, I can't afford it and second, I'm already milking as many cows as I can handle."

"But that's just it, Lissa," Travis pursued, "You're not alone. I'm here and Gus, and even Kenny helps."

"Travis, it'll be years before Kenny is any real help. Gus is trying to retire—and you?" She faltered. "You...well...don't you have to get back to your job one of these days?"

There! It was out—the question she'd been wanting to ask him for so long. He'd explained he was on a medical leave of absence, but surely he'd be returning to his engineering firm soon. She had ample proof that he was completely healed.

He crammed his hands in his pockets and took several more steps alongside her before he spoke. "Yes, I have a job waiting for me."

"Well?"

"Well what?"

"When are you leaving?"

"Do you want me to leave?"

Now what was she supposed to say? *No, I don't want you to leave? I love you desperately?* How could she tell him that when he'd revealed so little of his own feelings? She tripped as her heel caught in one of the deep ruts in the driveway.

Travis caught her before she fell. Doggedly, he demanded an answer. "Do you want me to leave?"

"That's not up to me," she stated truthfully. "It's up to you."

His eyes bore into her face, searching but not finding what he wanted. "I don't think so. I think it's all up to you. Do you want me as your lover, or don't you?"

Put like that, Melissa could give him only one answer. Of course she wanted him as her lover—but there was so much more. She wanted him as a partner, a friend, a father to her child. It appeared that he saw their relationship on only one level, the physical. "No," she answered firmly.

The short negative reply stunned him. Travis felt as he had when he'd been a boy and the love he had sought from his parents had been shrugged off as inconsequential. He covered his hurt with arrogance. "You do want me, Lissa. Want what I can do for you. You can't deny what happened when we made love. Are you telling me you don't need that?"

She squirmed in his arms, but he wouldn't let her go. "I've lived without a man for over a year, Travis. You don't have to stick around to soothe the frustrated widow. I can live without sex." With a violent twist of her shoulders she broke away from him.

Travis was furious. Without blinking an eye, she'd crushed every one of his idyllic dreams. He couldn't believe she'd deny what they had together. Lashing out, he said, "You were more than ready for me last night, and if I wanted to I could make you ready for me again right now."

Melissa was shocked. This was not the gentle lover she had given herself to last night but a crude stranger. She was lucky she'd discovered this part of him now before she'd committed herself any further.

"Damn you," he grated raggedly. "I know you need a man."

"Maybe so, but not a man like you." Her tone was flat. "Go back to your job, Travis. If you stick around much longer, the rumors will fly and I don't need that, either. My reputation means too much to me."

"It obviously means more to you than I do," he bit out. "I hope your precious reputation keeps you warm at night."

"A lot warmer than sex without love," she shot back. "And that's all you're capable of offering."

"You've got more of me than I've ever given to anybody," he exploded.

"Then you don't give enough of yourself, Travis." Her tone was sad. She'd given her heart once, and she was a fool for having done it again.

"Lissa, I didn't hold back anything when I made love to you."

Melissa's body became rigid. Travis just didn't understand and maybe he never would. "Neither did I, but sex isn't everything."

They stared into each other's eyes. Every fiber of Melissa's being longed for him not to leave her, to love her as she loved him. Travis made no move to stop her when she could stand it no longer and stepped away. Striding briskly down the walk toward her house, she forced herself to call back over her shoulder, pain and finality in the two short words. "Goodbye, Travis."

The lights from Gus's pickup truck outlined the departing Melissa and Travis's motionless form as he stood watching her. "Just finishing up?" Gus called loudly as he got out of his pickup, but the slamming of Melissa's back door was his only answer. "Does she have her back up over something?"

Travis sighed wearily, and reached into his shirt pocket for a cigarette. Without realizing how much he was revealing, he gritted through clenched teeth, "That woman could drive a man to drink."

Gus chuckled in male commiseration, unaware that what had transpired between Travis and Melissa was more than a simple spat. "Women can do that, all right. That's why I'm still a bachelor."

He lifted a mason jar out of the paper bag he carried. "Come on inside. I've got just the ticket, here. Frank's applejack. He can't get his sausage right, but this brew of his has a little oomph."

"Fine." Travis shrugged his shoulders and followed Gus into the house. "I could sure use something tonight."

Inside the kitchen Gus poured them each a plastic tumbler full of the hard cider. To his surprise Travis found that Frank's homemade applejack had more than "a little oomph"—it packed one helluva wallop. After his third glass of the potent concoction, Travis was so disoriented he would have spilled his guts to the devil and didn't have a chance against Gus's well-meaning interrogation.

Gus leaned back in his chair, a complacent grin on his face. "I knew she was the reason you haven't left yet, son. Got her hooks into you good, has she?"

Travis didn't particularly like Gus's choice of metaphor, but he had to admit it was an apt description. Up until a few minutes ago, he'd felt a lot like a flailing fish being played in by an expert angler. He'd almost reached the point where the net was looking good, but rather than reeling him in all the way, Melissa had cut the line.

"Not anymore," he admitted broodingly. "She threw me back."

"Horse feathers!" Gus refilled Travis's glass. "Mel's got enough sense to recognize a good catch. You must've done something wrong. She's a straightforward woman, and if you deal straight with her, things'll work out. Why don't you just come out with it?"

"What?" A perplexed furrow creased Travis's forehead, and he made an ineffective swipe at the stubborn hank of hair that kept getting in his eyes. The movement nearly cost him his balance, and he grabbed on to the table to keep from falling on the floor.

"This stuff must be a hundred proof," he mumbled, trying not to sway as he righted himself. He strained to keep his eyes focused on his uncle, who was fast becoming an indistinct blur.

"Marry her and be done with it. You don't fool with a woman like her."

Even in his increasingly befuddled state, Travis realized that Gus assumed he and Melissa were a matched set. As far as he could recall, he had never said or done anything in front of Gus for him to reach that conclusion. "No, you don't," Travis agreed remorsefully as his heavy lids fell over his eyes. "But she doesn't want me, so who needs her?"

The next thing Travis knew, Gus was helping him toward his bedroom. He grunted at the twinge of pain in his side as Gus let him drop on the bed.

"Don't make the same mistake I did boy. It's no good living your life alone. Don't pass up the chance for a woman like Mel. There aren't many like her."

"Nobody like her," Travis declared bleakly as he burrowed his head in the pillow.

TRAVIS LEANED OVER THE TOILET, waiting to regain his breath before attempting to get back on his feet. It took him a full five minutes before he was confident of his ability to stagger unaided back to bed. Stretched out on the mattress, he slowly opened one eye, praying that the swirling stucco pattern on the ceiling wouldn't incite another bout of nausea. When he was absolutely certain that he wasn't going to be sick again, he opened his other eye.

A bright beam of sun from the unshaded window was tormenting him. It bored into his face like a sharp spike. He knew he wasn't dead, but he wanted to die. He'd had a few hangovers in his life, but never anything like this. It was her. Melissa had done this to him. His guts twisted with the knowledge that the woman had gotten to him so badly that he'd not only started smoking again but had willingly consumed an enormous amount of some noxious poison, innocently labeled cider.

Travis had imbibed some of the most exotic drinks the world had to offer, and none of them had even come close to annihilating him as had Frank Kohler's applejack. He had new respect for his uncle. Sometime in the early morning, he'd heard Gus's off-key announcement, "I'm going to do chores, now." Travis hadn't even been able to lift his head off the pillow, let alone try making it to the barn.

He wondered if Melissa regretted his absence. Would she miss the morning greeting he'd promised to deliver each day? He doubted it. From what she'd said to him last night, she was probably glad he wasn't there to bother her.

The pain in his heart was more severe than the one in his head. He cursed his own stupidity. He knew better than to let himself care enough for someone to be hurt if they didn't return his affection. He'd tried so hard to make her fall in love with him, but obviously he hadn't been very successful. Otherwise, how could she want him to leave? If her feelings for him were strong enough, she'd have asked him to stay.

And what about his feelings for her? Was this tortuous misery love? If it was, he was sure he wanted nothing more to do with it. Unfortunately Melissa Lindstrand had gotten too far under his skin for him to walk away easily. He knew he'd enjoy working with her on the farm, helping to raise her son and taking the last bit of worry from her shoulders. But Melissa didn't want him.

He had promised his company that he'd return by the end of the week. There was a crew of men waiting for him in South America, a bridge needing to be rebuilt and there was no longer any reason to delay. Melissa was a strong, practical woman who could handle anything. He wasn't needed here. Wintersfield would do fine in her capable hands.

9

MELISSA LET THE RIPENED GRAIN SIFT through her fingers, then squinted up at the scorching summer sun. She didn't like the oppressive feel of the air, the tiny funnels of dust that swirled furiously at the end of each windrow. From past experience, she thought there should be some sign of an approaching storm, but there was hardly any wind and not a cloud in the sky. She tried to shrug off the anxious feeling as she surveyed the field of waiting oats. If the dry weather held, she'd be finished combining them by the end of the day. Before climbing back up into the air-conditioned cab of the combine, she turned her gaze toward the house.

She saw nothing that should have disturbed her, yet she had an uneasy sensation that something was wrong. Gus was sitting on the steps of her front porch throwing apples to Mitzi, who chased after them as if they were bouncing rubber balls. In the shade of the mammoth oak trees that grew between the two houses, she located Kenny. He was playing with his toy farm machinery in the large tractor wheel that served as his sandbox.

It was a typical August day, hot and humid. After a last look toward the house, Melissa took a swallow of water from her canteen, then climbed into the combine. During the next hour, she completed several rounds of the field without even being aware of it. As they'd been every day since he'd left, her thoughts were centered on Travis.

He'd have been in South America for close to two months now. Two weeks after he'd left, Gus had received a short letter that stated Travis had arrived at the bridge site and that the rebuilding project was already under way. The local government had assured the company that the area was now secured from further attack, but Melissa still worried.

The newspapers were always recounting some sudden revolution, some terrorist attack in South America. Even though she might never see Travis again, she couldn't bear the thought of his being injured or worse—killed. Though their parting had been anything but amiable, she still loved him, would always love him.

In his letter Travis had requested Gus write back and tell him all about the goings-on at the farm. He'd wanted to hear if Kenny had made any progress in learning to ride a two-wheeler. He had even asked about the health and well-being of the two calves he'd helped to deliver, but there'd been no inquiries concerning her. That had hurt and still did. She knew that he had put her totally out of his life, and that knowledge was a painful weight lodged in her chest. He hadn't even said goodbye to her.

Reaching the end of a row, Melissa felt unusually hot and turned off the engine. Even with her air-conditioning, the atmosphere inside the cab was stifling. Maybe there was a broken seal in the lines. She pulled down the side window and was hit in the face with a blast of moist heat. The reason it was getting so warm inside the cab was because the air outside was like that in the tropics.

As if the sound came from the bowels of the earth, she heard an ominous rumble. When she gazed toward the horizon, however, she saw only a harmless band of wispy white clouds. They looked like ghostly fingers pointing up to the fathomless blue sky. There had to be a storm coming, but there was no reason for concern yet. She should have plenty of time to finish harvesting the oats.

Quickly she closed the window, trying to keep as much cool air as possible from escaping the cab. Starting the powerful engine once more, she shifted into gear and began a new row. Perspiration dripped down her forehead and into her eyes. She wiped her forehead on her sleeve, but there was nothing she could do about the tiny rivers of sweat streaming between her breasts. Were these the conditions Travis worked under?

The atmosphere between her and Travis the day he had left had not been so very different than that of a gathering storm. The tension strung between them had been as heavy and heated as the hot humid air that surrounded the cab. They had behaved like opposing fronts, ready for a confrontation that had never occurred.

Travis's last words had been spoken with such cold finality that Melissa hadn't been able to utter a sound. He hadn't even been speaking to her but to Gus, explaining the reasons for his early departure. Nevertheless, the words had been for her. "I didn't intend to stay here this long. This was merely a stopover until I recuperated. I enjoyed my stay, Gus, but there's no longer any reason to put off going back to work. It's time for me to stop playing around."

In the weeks he'd been gone, Melissa had been forced to admit that she'd indulged in a meaningless summer fling with a man who'd never had any intention of letting it develop into something more. The passion he'd felt for her hadn't even lasted until the end of his stay. When he'd looked at her for the last time, his expression had been merely polite, almost indifferent. Those wondrous dark eyes that had so often filled with gold at the sight of her had been an even brown. The lips that had known every inch of her body had been drawn in a straight line. He'd shaken Gus's hand, given Kenny a warm hug, but all he'd imparted to her was a cool nod and "Thanks for everything, Melissa."

He had reason to thank her, all right. She *had* given him everything. Her body and her heart had been his to do with as he wished—and he had chosen to walk away.

The night before his departure, she'd cried herself to sleep, more grief-stricken then she'd been even after Gordy had died. She had given Travis a chance to tell her that she meant something to him, but all he had talked about was how good they were together in bed. Being his lover was wonderful, but she wanted to be his wife. He'd been good with Kenny, had seemed to enjoy working on the farm, and she had fooled herself into thinking that he might consider making his life with her. He might have wanted a home for a few pleasant days, but he couldn't commit himself to her permanently, couldn't put down such deep roots.

Gus had guessed the cause of her depression and

had tried to make excuses for Travis. Unfortunately they made sense. Travis had never really had a home and had spent his whole life traveling, first from one boarding school to the next and then in his job. His parents had taught him not to count on anyone but himself, and he couldn't trust that someone might want him forever. The summer vacations Travis had spent at Wintersfield had been the only times he had lived within a family atmosphere.

Both Gus and his parents had loved and wanted Travis, but when they had offered to keep him until he graduated from high school, Geoffrey Winters had not allowed it. According to Gus, Geoff and Priscilla felt it was socially acceptable to tuck their son away in various expensive boarding schools, but it wouldn't reflect well on them to leave him on the family farm. Loving grandparents, a place to call his own, weren't nearly as important in his parents' eyes as the strict discipline and excellent education Travis would receive in private schools.

If only she had known more about his background before he had left, she would have understood his motives better and wouldn't have let herself in for so much hurt. She now realized that the hungry look in his eyes had been caused by a short-lived envy for the kind of relationship she had with Kenny, Gus and her entire family.

For a brief time, Melissa surmised, Travis had mistakenly decided that he wanted family ties, but it hadn't taken him long to realize that he was happier on his own. She knew him well enough to realize that when he really wanted something, he went after it with single-minded purpose. If he'd wanted her brand of love, he would have stayed at Wintersfield or taken her with him.

After completing the last round, Melissa maneuvered the combine toward the track leading back to the machine shed. The sky had grown darker and although still blue, it wasn't the right color blue for a typical summer day. Glancing up, she frowned at the peculiar slate gray, almost green shade that now hovered threateningly over the land. Looking toward the west, she saw with alarm that the wispy fingers of white had been replaced by a boiling roll of clouds that resembled the pounding surf on the ocean's shore.

In the time it took for her to shift into a higher gear and drive a few yards farther along the track, the boiling white cloud had consumed half the sky. Hurtling behind the front was a black sheet of suppressed power that obliterated the sun, driving relentlessly closer. One minute she felt certain she'd make the machine shed before the rain and the next she wasn't certain of anything but acute danger. It was three o'clock in the afternoon, but it was as dark as midnight. This was not a mere summer thunderstorm but a full-blown monster intent on devouring everything in its path.

The combine shuddered under the first rush of wind and Melissa realized, as heavy as the piece of machinery was, it could be blown over and she could be crushed beneath it. She had to get out, get away. Fighting the malevolent force that pushed against the door, she finally managed to get it open and flung herself onto the ground.

With growing terror, she saw the mind-boggling

image of full-grown trees, large sheets of metal and
pieces of wood flying like feathers through the air.
She felt like Dorothy in *The Wizard of Oz* watching
her world as it floated past her bedroom window.
Clawing the ground with her fingers so she wouldn't
be swept away like everything else, Melissa dragged
herself toward a ditch.

Headfirst, she dived into the gully that bordered
the track. Melissa flattened herself against the ground
and covered her head with her arms. Insanely, she
raged at the storm as she squeezed her eyes shut
against the flying debris. She knew they sometimes
occurred, but August wasn't tornado season! Why
didn't the storm know that!

As if nature were making a concession for the old
occurrence, there was no twisting black funnel, but a
straight-lined wind that raced furiously across the
open farmland. The sound was loud and awesome,
causing Melissa to shudder in terror. It was like lying beneath a trestle while a speeding locomotive
roared overhead within inches of her prone form.

Kenny! My God, Kenny, she sobbed, picturing her
small son as she had last seen him, playing uncon-
cernedly in his sandbox. Had Gus been able to reach
him in time? Were they both safe? Could they possibly have made it to the storm cellar before the wind?
There was nothing she could do. She couldn't move,
was being relentlessly held to the ground by the
hand of a spiteful demon.

As fast as it had come, the storm was over. And
then the rains came. A deluge of water gushed from
the heavens. It was so dense she couldn't see more
than a foot in front of her face. The dry earth be-

neath her wouldn't accept the water, and the gully was no longer a sanctuary. She righted herself and scrambled out of the fast-filling ditch. Stumbling through the sheets of rain, she staggered toward the farmhouse. It was so dark, the rain so heavy that she couldn't see, but instinct directed her feet.

She had to get to Kenny, find Gus. Cutting across a field, she encountered a row of boards and was momentarily disoriented. There shouldn't have been a fence there. Was she lost? No, to her horror she realized it wasn't a fence but a line of jagged boards that the wind had pummeled into the wounded earth.

She heard Gus calling her name and the sound of his voice filled her with incredible relief. If he was safe, so was Kenny. She knew he would have died before letting anything happen to her little boy. She ran faster, returning his call and using his response as a directional guide.

Moments later, she threw open the screen door of Gus's porch and fell into his waiting arms. Kenny threw himself at her and she sank to the floor, hugging him to her breast. "Oh baby, oh baby. Thank God, you're okay," she cried as her fingers gave his sturdy limbs and torso a quick once over.

As she assured herself that Kenny was all right, Mitzi bounded across the porch and began licking her face. For once, she didn't reprimand the effusive pet for this form of greeting. Instead Melissa wrapped one arm around the dog's neck and returned its affection.

"It's creepy in that old cellar, mom," Kenny complained, his voice muffled against her bosom. "But I was sure glad we were down in there, even if we did have only one measly candle." His little body shook slightly as he valiantly tried to maintain a brave front. "You should've been with us, mom," he accused, his arms taking a death grip around her neck. "You made me all worried!"

Although Gus was less verbal with his concern, his large hand never left her shoulder. Melissa patted his hand, certifying that she was all right, then leaned back on her heels. She took Kenny's face in her hands. "I was worried, too, honey. It came up so fast, I couldn't get out of the field. I ended up laying in the ditch and that was creepy, too."

"Showed good sense," Gus said gruffly. He squeezed her shoulder and brushed a trace of betraying moisture away from his eyes. "Hope those blasted cows haven't hightailed it across the county. I'll bet this blower busted the pasture fence. We'd best get out there and round 'em up. We lost power, and there's no telling when we'll get it back. Tonight we'll be milking by hand."

Melissa groaned and reached for one of the rain slickers always hung in the porch, then laughed. "I'm already wet to the skin. Guess this won't help much now."

"It's almost stopped raining. Why don't you run next door and get into some dry clothes," Gus suggested. "Kenny and I'll wait for you here."

"What about the house?" Melissa asked. "Did you lose any windows? I saw whole trees flying through the air."

"We just got out of the cellar," Gus admitted, scratching his head as if she'd reminded him of something he hadn't yet thought of. "I haven't even checked." His expression was confounded. "I figured if the porch was standing, so was the rest of the house."

While they stood in the porch, a curtain seemed to lift outside. Rain continued to drip from the eaves, but the sun began showing through the clouds. "Strangest storm I ever saw," Gus remarked just before his jaw went slack. "My stars, Mel! The garage ain't there."

Completely dumbfounded, Melissa stared through the screen at the empty concrete foundation. If the garage was gone, what else was gone? Evidently Gus was having the same thought.

They both rushed outside. Looking first toward the main house, the only damage they saw was a few missing shingles and one broken window on the second floor. Between the two houses, however, the majestic oaks that had lived for more than a century lay in broken disarray, their massive trunks split at disjointed angles, their groundless roots yanked cruelly from the earth.

A sick feeling permeated Melissa's body as she surveyed the huge tree trunk that lay over the sandbox. The sudden image she had was too terrible to contemplate, and she forced it out of her mind.

"My beautiful trees," Gus mourned.

"I'm so sorry," Melissa consoled.

Those steadfast trees had been a symbol of the strength and permanency of Wintersfield. They had provided loving shelter, stood like sentinels along the walk that led to the main house. They had seemed part of the land that would go on forever, but within seconds they had been destroyed. Now they looked like match sticks discarded by the forces of nature. Melissa had never been more aware of her own mortality. She felt small and humble, incredibly fragile.

As if mourning a human loss, she put her arms around Gus. His shoulders were shaking and he seemed suddenly frail, as if he had aged ten years in ten minutes. Clinging to each other in a mutual expression of grief, they strove for the strength to face whatever else was to come. "We all made it through this, Gus," Melissa reassured gently. "We can face anything else. Things can be replaced."

"Not trees." Kenny slipped his hand into his mother's, his usual ebullience dampened. "God makes trees." His lower lip quivered as he pointed to the end of the drive.

Melissa's gaze followed his outstretched arm. "Oh no," she moaned.

There was no barn. There was nothing but a pile of rubble. The roof of the machine shed was tilted into the ground. The far wall had caved in on the tractors and equipment. Even as they stood there, trying to assimilate their shock, the dazed cows began milling into the cow yard. It was the sound of their bawling that spurred Melissa and eventually Gus into action.

The next few hours went by quickly. The power company was the first to arrive, followed by the state highway patrol, fire trucks, local news personnel and an army of friends, neighbors and relatives. The freak storm had centered its fury on Wintersfield, and even those farms located not far down the road had completely escaped damage. Melissa felt it was a stroke of fate, as if her dream had been deliberately snatched away. There was nothing else to do but start over, and she didn't know if that would be possible.

Melissa knew that, like most farmers, Gus was underinsured. He might be forced to sell the herd because there was nowhere to milk them. Oddly enough, the only machine to escape damage was the combine, and there would be no harvest, since the crops had been destroyed. What had started out as a most promising year had ended in a total loss.

"HONEY, WHY DON'T YOU COME HOME with me," Elaine Kvam coaxed, slipping her arm reassuringly around Melissa's waist. "There's nothing else you can do here tonight."

"Thanks, mom," Melissa answered wearily. "I appreciate your sending Kenny home with Burt and Sharon. But I want to stay here. I'm worried about Gus. Look at him, mom. He seems so lost."

Gus stood at the front window, gazing outside at the blinking lanterns in the barnyard. His eyes appeared haunted. He kept wringing his hands and muttering to himself.

"I can't leave him alone," Melissa murmured.

"This is hard for any of us to believe, but it must be doubly hard on Gus. He was born here. I don't think he's ever been much farther than the county line. Maybe you should call his family, Melissa," Elaine advised. "Or would you rather I did it?"

"None of them would come, mom." Melissa ignored her mother's all-seeing eyes. "From what Gus has told me about his brother, he cares nothing for the farm. Since Gus wasn't hurt, there's nothing to tell him."

"What about Travis?" Elaine persisted. "You can't tell me he doesn't care."

Melissa successfully avoided the subject of Travis by saying, "I have to get back outside. I only came in to get a cup of coffee. It will be hours yet before the milking is done."

For the rest of the night, Melissa was so busy that she couldn't think about anything but what needed to be done. She and her neighbors worked far into the night. Even when her generous volunteers had gone home to bed, Melissa remained awake. There was too much to do, too much to think about. She couldn't afford the luxury of sleep.

After making sure Gus had gone to bed, Melissa sat down at the large rolltop desk in his living room. She pulled out the stock records and insurance policies, made a list of places she would have to telephone in the morning and spent the rest of the night trying to itemize the damage.

It was an overwhelming task. The agent had told her she had to be specific, must remember to list every item contained in the garage, barn, machine shed and chicken house. She began with the chickens, for they were the only lives that had been lost. A morbid laugh bubbled between her lips.

"Stupid birds! Should've flown the coop at the first sign of trouble." Melissa was getting slaphappy if this was an example of her humor. She sobered as she was hit with another thought. Wouldn't Travis laugh if he could see her now? At the moment, she would have given anything to hold on to those calves—his "babies." She didn't want to be practical any more. Those calves weren't dollars and cents, but a part of her family that she was being forced to sell.

The next day Melissa was so busy she could justify ignoring her mother's suggestion to call Travis. When the cows were loaded onto the trucks and driven away, however, Gus cried, and Melissa realized she could not delay the phone call much longer. When the bulldozers arrived to raze the barn, she knew the time had come.

As the grinding engines leveled the broken fragments of Gus's family heritage, the older man sank more and more deeply into a depression. Melissa couldn't get through to him, and she was faced with making necessary decisions. Although she had been working toward ownership, she still didn't feel she had the right to decide the destiny of Wintersfield. Someone had told her in no uncertain terms, "this place is owned by a Winters, and it always will be." That someone needed to know what had happened. No matter how much pain it would cause her, she'd have to place that call.

She located Travis's letter in Gus's desk, took down the number on the letterhead and dialed Rogers Engineering. After explaining the emergency, she was given the information she needed.

Melissa was dozing in a rocking chair, in the wee hours of the morning, an afghan wrapped around her cramped body, when the overseas operator's message came through. Her party was waiting, she was told. All she could hear was a static crackle.

Then, a low-timbred voice shouted over the inter-
ference on the line, "What's wrong, Lissa!"

Melissa had promised herself not to lose her composure. But, with the first word he uttered, a harsh,
burning ache closed her throat. Silent tears began
falling and built into sobs when Travis started
shouting.

"My God, Lissa. Answer me! I know you're there.
Is it Gus?" His rapid-fire demands were filled with
anxiety.

"You... you have to come home, Travis," she
wailed, incoherently. "It's all gone! Everything's
gone."

"What do you mean? What's gone?" Travis's tone
was edged with panic. After a pause he said more
gently, "Come on, honey, tell me what's going on."

Unable to stop herself, Melissa began to babble.
"They said it was a hundred fifty miles an hour. It
blew everything down. We had to sell all the cows,
and Gus couldn't take that," she sobbed. "I... we...
Gus needs you."

"What was it, Lissa, a tornado? Were you hurt?
Was anyone hurt?" Travis spoke slowly, as if speaking to a hysteric. "Is Kenny all right? Is Gus all
right?"

"None of us are all right," she cried with irra-
tional annoyance. What was the matter with him!
Why did he think she was calling? "Don't you understand? We lost Wintersfield. Gus broke down
and cried. I haven't seen Kenny in two days, and I
haven't slept since it happened. The window broke,
and the rain ruined my grandmother's tatted bed-

spread. That can't be replaced, Travis. And the oak trees, Travis."

"Dammit, Lissa!" he bellowed. "I don't care about the oak trees or your grandmother's bedspread! Why haven't you seen Kenny? Where the hell is he?"

"He's with Burt and Sharon," she explained calmly, sniffling. "I can't have him here. There were live wires everywhere. Now there's too much to do. Don't you understand, Travis?"

"Lissa, get a grip on yourself," he ordered her in a tone that made her gulp. "I'll be there as soon as I can."

She reacted to the command in his voice as anyone with an ounce of sense would. Travis had taken over, and the relief she felt stilled her trembling. When she spoke again, it was with some degree of calm. "Thank you, Travis. I'm fine, but your uncle really needs you."

She heard a humorless chuckle, then, "Sure you are. I could tell that as soon as I heard your calm voice."

"I'm just a little upset, that's all!" she retorted, indignantly.

"It would kill you to admit that you need me, wouldn't it?"

"I do need you," she protested. "I can't make any more of these decisions by myself. I don't own Wintersfield, and Gus isn't in his right mind."

"What?" The fear was back in his voice.

Hastily she amended, "I mean I'm worried about him. This is too much for someone his age to cope with. My mother said I should call you."

"Thank God for that," he swore quietly. "You sit tight, and don't do anything until I get there. Is that clear?"

Melissa was insulted by his domineering tone. "What do you think I'm going to do? Sell the farm out from underneath Gus before you get here?"

There was a long, ominous silence. Melissa was halfway afraid he'd hung up on her until he spoke again. She could almost picture him, brushing back the hair over his forehead in exasperation when he replied, "I'm going to forget you said that, since you're obviously overwrought. Now you listen to me. I've had all I'm going to take from you, lady. It took me two hours to get to a phone and another two to get the connection. I'll be damned if I'm going to argue with you about anything right now. We have a lot to settle between us, Lissa, and you can be damned sure we will when I get there. Now is there anything else you want to say to me before I hang up this phone?"

Melissa bit her tongue. She wasn't the only one who was overwrought. "When can Gus expect you?"

"You can expect me in a couple of days," he retorted. After a short pause, his voice came again, raw with emotion. "Lissa, I have to know. Is everyone okay? No one was hurt?"

"We're all fine."

10

THE SCAVENGER WORE A GREEN POLYESTER SUIT and an ingratiating smile. The only delineation between his chest and belly was a belt that cinched his girth so tightly he reminded Melissa of an overstuffed pillow with a string tied around its middle. "We'll offer you a hundred thousand for this place," Ralph Jenkins of Jenkins & Willoughby Developers boasted proudly, as if he'd just presented Melissa with a priceless gift. "We'll take it off your hands, and you won't have to be bothered with cleaning up this mess."

"That's not my decision, Mr. Jenkins," Melissa countered wearily. "I'm not the owner, and he's not available right now."

A touch of belligerence stole into the man's sharp eyes. His thick jowls creased with his ingratiating smile. "You'd be doing him a favor if you convince him to talk to me. This kind of offer won't come along every day." Jenkins's tone became wheedling. "I've even been authorized to go up a few thousand if Winters agrees today. We don't do that for everybody, but we understand this has been a rough time for you.

"Jenkins and Willoughby wants to make things as easy as possible for folks that have suffered such tragedy. I know you've probably been contacted by other firms, but we try to look out for the little guy. We won't take advantage of you."

The rage that Melissa couldn't suppress was apparent in her eyes as she stated coldly, "Of course not, Mr. Jenkins. That's why you're offering half what this place is worth. I'll give Gus your message, but it won't do any good. I suggest you get back in your car and get off the property." Jenkins was the latest in a drove of eager opportunists who had swarmed over Wintersfield since the storm.

After dealing with the first round of fast-talking con men who appeared only hours after the devastation, Melissa was no longer shocked, but angry. "I don't have time to listen to any more of this," she dismissed.

He refused to leave, however, insisting that she deliver his offer to Gus immediately. "You won't get a better deal somewhere else, you know." Jenkins then proceeded to launch his second wave of attack, and other than bodily removing him, Melissa had no choice but to listen.

Melissa, now trapped outside Gus's porch, was the last barrier to his getting inside—and she absolutely refused to subject Gus to one of these vultures. The older man was still in a state of shock and in no condition to have to listen while an unfeeling stranger bargained for his heritage. Eventually Gus might very well have to sell the farm since it would cost so much to rebuild, but it was far too soon for him to consider making that kind of decision.

Out of the corner of her eye, Melissa saw a whirl of dust coming closer and closer along the gravel road. Memories of another summer day returned in a rush. Only one person drove that way—Travis. It had been over forty-eight hours since she'd talked to him, the longest two days of her life.

Jenkins's syrupy voice faded away as Melissa recalled the phone conversation that had precipitated Travis's arrival. She'd made a total fool out of herself, broken down completely and sobbed like a baby. It was just that she'd been so tired, so incredibly tired. If he hadn't said anything, hadn't called her "Lissa" in that husky drawl of his, she might have been able to remain calm.

Even now, tears smarted behind her eyes as she watched the late-model car career into the drive and screech to a halt before the empty foundation that had recently supported the garage. She didn't know how she was going to handle seeing Travis again, but couldn't deny the overwhelming sense of relief that swept through her as he climbed out of the car and began walking toward her. Even though his expression reminded her of an avenging angel, he was a damned welcome sight. Dressed in a rumpled short-sleeved khaki shirt and pants that had seen far better days, sporting a two-days' growth of beard, he still exuded strength and vitality.

TRAVIS HAD NEVER HAD THIS GUT-WRENCHING FEELING before. Melissa looked like hell, but to him she was the most beautiful sight in the world. Her dirty blue jeans and wrinkled knit top were in even worse condition than his sorry clothes. But it wasn't the state of her clothing that concerned him. It was the purple shadows that lay like dark feathers beneath her large blue eyes. Her healthy complexion was covered by an ashen mask, her blond hair hung in limp strands, her proud shoulders drooped with fatigue. But all that mattered to him was that she appeared to be all in one piece.

He didn't know what he would have done if anything had happened to her. He had thought of nothing else since her frantic phone call that had affected him more powerfully than anything in his life. His strong, practical Melissa had been out of control, unable to cope. She needed him! He couldn't get here fast enough, and every delay fed his anxiety.

Blue eyes searched and found brown ones, sending a message that Travis couldn't misunderstand. All the pain, grief and fatigue she had endured for the last several days was there in her eyes.

"Travis," she whispered and stepped toward him, completely forgetting Ralph Jenkins's presence. "Thank God you're here."

The clawlike grip she suddenly felt on her arm barely registered until Melissa found she couldn't move. Dumbly she turned her head toward her captor. Jenkins's demeanor had undergone a dramatic change. His eyes were narrowed into irritated slits, his complexion mottled with angry red.

"Just a minute, girlie. You're not talking to anybody else until you've taken my offer in to the old man. This is a damned good deal, and by God he's going to hear it right now. I'm through pussyfooting around."

"Take your hand off me," Melissa grated, and tried to shake free but Jenkins only tightened his grip.

"Not until you take me inside," Jenkins snarled.

"Do what she says, mister," Travis advised in a dangerously quiet voice as he came to stand beside Melissa.

"You don't know what's going on here," Jenkins persisted. Sensing that Melissa was not going to change her mind, he appealed to the newcomer on the scene. "If you've got any pull with this stubborn woman, you'll tell her not to look a gift horse in the mouth. I'm offering cold cash for this place, and she won't even let me in to see Winters. The old man might be a bit addled right now, but he won't thank you for passing up my deal."

With a glare, Travis took a step forward. "This place isn't for sale."

Overlooking the finality in Travis's words, Jenkins appeared to be grateful he was now dealing with a man. "Every man's got a price, buddy," he said companionably. "We both know that." Speculation gleamed in his eyes as he appraised Travis. "You look like you could use a few extra bucks. Maybe you and me can strike a deal. I don't know who you are, but if you can help me convince Winters to take what I'm offering, there might be something in it for you."

Melissa felt as if everything was happening in slow motion. Travis's arm came back. His hand formed into a fist. Like a battering ram, the arm drove forward in a direct line with Jenkins's chin. The man's body lifted up into the air with the force of the blow, then descended like a deflated balloon. Seconds later, everything speeded up again and Jenkins was half crawling, half running toward his car.

Holding his sore jaw, he waited until he was a safe

distance away before shaking his fist. "You'll be sorry for this! You haven't heard the last from Ralph Jenkins."

"Want to make a bet?" Travis menaced beneath his breath, his gaze never wavering until the man was inside his car and pulling out of the drive.

Jenkins's comical retreat brought a semihysterical laugh to Melissa's lips, but it died after one look at Travis's face. His anger hadn't abated after Jenkins's departure. His brown eyes drilled into her face, and Melissa stepped nervously out of his reach.

She was pinned by the primitive force of Travis's gaze. "You look like hell," he accused. "What the devil have you done to yourself?"

"It's nice seeing you again, too!" she shot back, bravely.

She had thought Travis had stepped in to save her from the obnoxious developer but now felt anything but safe when he took a similarly tight grip on her elbow.

"Take me to Gus. I want to make sure he's all right before I talk with you," he insisted.

Ordinarily Melissa would have put up more of a fight, but today she just wasn't up to it. Her shoulders slumped further as Travis pushed her through the doorway. She didn't say a word while he bodily escorted her into the kitchen but flared briefly when he shoved her down in a chair. "Don't push me around, Travis! I—"

"Sit down," Travis commanded sharply, and Melissa complied. She was drained, didn't have the strength for another confrontation this morning, and Travis was obviously ready to thwart any sign of rebellion.

Gus was seated at the kitchen table staring morosely into his coffee and even with all the commotion didn't look up until Travis placed a hand on his shoulder. "I'm here, Uncle Gus," he said gently. "Everything's going to be all right."

Melissa could not believe her eyes. Gus immediately brightened. After all of her efforts, her undeniable concern for him, it had taken Travis only a few words to accomplish what she'd been trying to do for days. Thank God she'd swallowed her pride, called Travis and gotten him back here. Gus had definitely needed his nephew and—well, maybe she did too, at least until things were back under control.

"I knew you'd be here," Gus revealed with a weak smile. "Isn't this the damnedest thing? A man and his fathers before him work from dawn until dusk all of their lives and with two blinks the whole thing blows away. I'm too old to start over, and Mel can't afford to buy me out. We're in one helluva pickle."

"The land's still here and I'm buying you out," Travis informed them coolly, shocking both Melissa and Gus. "There's nothing for you to worry about. By next year this place will be better than it was. That's a promise."

"You mean it, boy?" Gus asked, his voice filled with both hope and disbelief. "I don't think you've thought this through. It'll take a heap of money to rebuild. I'm not even sure if it's worth it. Getting started in today's economy might be a fool's dream."

"Oh, I'm a fool, all right," Travis admitted, self-mockingly. "I was a fool to leave when I did. Believe me, everything'll work out. I'm too tired to talk about it right now and by the looks of you two, you're not much better off. Go to bed, Uncle Gus. We'll talk more later."

Casting Melissa a warning glance that told her that if she moved, she'd regret it, Travis helped a weary but hopeful Gus to his bedroom. Moments later, Travis came back for her.

"I'm putting you to bed, Lissa. Let's go." He pulled her out of the chair and started for the door. He led her firmly down the porch steps and toward her own house. He stopped when he saw the first fallen tree. "Good Lord!" he breathed harshly, stopping abruptly to survey the shambles around them.

With as much interest as she could muster, when all she really wanted to do was close her eyes and go to sleep, Melissa watched his reaction. Evidently, he hadn't really taken a good look when he'd arrived, but now he saw everything. Travis stood with mouth slack, feet apart and eyes wide as they darted from one disastrous sight to the next.

"No wonder you were hysterical," he said softly, more to himself than to her. He gathered her into his arms. "Where were you and Kenny when this was happening?" he whispered into her hair. He wanted to comfort her, rock her in his arms, impart some of his strength to her. Standing amidst the rubble of her broken dreams, his family's severed roots, they were the only reality left in a world that had gone haywire.

He felt her delicate shudder, her weakness and

knew that now was not the time to show her how desperately he wanted her. Yet, when he tried to let her go, she clung to him.

"Oh, Travis," Melissa whimpered. "I didn't think you'd ever get here. I need you so much."

It was all Travis needed to hear. Now he knew she would not reject him, but he wanted her to be fully recovered before showing her the intensity of his feelings. She was like a limp doll in his arms. Slowly he let her go—first her hair, then, very reluctantly, the body contact that had fused them.

"I've been worried sick about you. You sounded half-crazy on the phone, and I thought I'd lose my mind before I got here."

Melissa's heart swelled within her at the sound of the fear in his voice, but she didn't have the strength to respond. Being held in his arms was a comfort and that was all she needed or wanted right now. Even the sharp scrape of his beard was soothing, further proof that she was no longer alone. She let the tears fall, knowing she could finally let go. Travis's strength allowed her the freedom to give up her burden.

She had been giving, giving, giving for days and now she needed to take. Although she was thrilled by the soft light in his eyes and the knowledge that he cared about her, she needed what little energy she had to remain standing. Even her skin ached, and her neck felt too weak to go on holding up her head.

Travis lifted his hand to brush the hair away from her forehead, his fingers trembling as he wiped away her tears. "Oh, sweetheart, don't cry. You're not alone anymore."

Melissa let out a long ragged sigh. "Thank you. I just can't handle this by myself any more."

"Tell me where you were when it happened." he asked tenderly, his lips buried in her hair.

Melissa swayed forward and wrapped her arms around his waist for support. In a hollow voice she gave him a brief summary of everyone's whereabouts during the storm. "All in all, I guess we were very lucky."

"All in all, I guess we were," Travis agreed softly, hugging her tightly. "I'm surprised the houses are still standing."

Melissa's answering nod was barely perceptible. "We only lost a few shingles and some windows. Dad and Burt managed to get them boarded up...." Her voice trailed off. She could no longer resist the urge to rest her head on his shoulder, close her eyes and relinquish the burden she'd carried for what seemed like forever.

Just a little while, she thought. *I'll rest here for just a little while and then go back to work. I don't have to do it all myself, Travis is here.* Sleepily she breathed in the smell that was uniquely his, reassuring herself that he was real, was holding her and wasn't going to disappear if she opened her eyes.

"You're out on your feet. Let's get you to bed," he muttered brokenly.

Her eyes shot open and she pulled away. "I can't do that yet. There's so much that has to be done, and there'll be more people coming here like Jenkins. They've come down on the farm like a swarm of locusts, offering to buy everything for pennies. Someone has to keep them away from Gus. It's disgusting, and I won't have them badgering him.

"My folks'll be here after chores. Dad and my brothers are going to saw up the trees. I have to feed them and—"

"You don't have to do anything but get some rest and I'm going to make certain you do exactly that." As if he weren't suffering the same degree of exhaustion, Travis lifted her off her feet.

Maybe she should have protested, but it felt so wonderful to let him take over. Travis sidestepped the fallen trees and branches and carried her the rest of the way to her house. He didn't put her down until after he'd mounted the stairs and brought her into the bedroom.

Taking a swift glance around the room, he surveyed the provincial maple furnishings, heavy cotton drapes and the large, Oriental rug that covered most of the polished wood floor. "Nice," he acknowledged as he lowered her to her feet. "I'm going to like this room." His hands moved to the buttons of her blouse.

He had unfastened three buttons before she found her voice. "Stop that. What *are* you doing?"

"What does it look like?" he asked impatiently. "I'm taking these clothes off you. You won't need them for the next few hours."

He brushed her hands aside and continued undressing her. Using the advantage of his greater strength, he urged her into compliance. Within moments she was stripped down to her panties and bra.

"How can you have sex on your mind at a time like this?" she cried desperately as his fingers unclasped her bra and threw it onto the floor.

His answer came from somewhere by her knees as he pulled the last remaining garment down her trembling legs. "It might be on my mind, sweetheart, but that's as far as it goes. You give me more credit than I deserve."

He swept the covers back and pushed her down on the mattress. "The mind may be willing but the flesh is weak. I've gone without sleep for two days now, and I'm just too damned tired to do anything but hold my woman in my arms and pass out."

He pulled the covers up to her chin and said sternly, "I have a few things to take care of and then I'll be back. Don't you dare get out of this bed until I tell you to." He turned on his heel and was gone.

Melissa struggled futilely with the countless things she had wanted to say to him. There was so much unresolved between them, but he was behaving as if everything was settled. Her brain might be fuzzy, her reactions slow but she did know she shouldn't have allowed him to get away with half the high-handed things he'd done since his return. Apparently, he had no question about her status. As far as he was concerned, she was his woman. At the moment, that sounded pretty good to her, too, but tomorrow she was going to get a further explanation.

Yes. Tomorrow she'd tell him he couldn't order her around. Tomorrow she'd find out just what he meant when he said she was his woman. Tomorrow she'd deal with his announcement that he was buying Wintersfield and rebuilding it. But for now, the feel of the smooth, clean sheets was so good. The mattress had never felt so soft, and her body had never felt so boneless....

Her eyelids closed, only fluttered briefly when some time later she felt a dip in the mattress and a large body slip into her bed. "Go away," she mumbled. "You can't sleep with me. My mother—"

"Knows where I am," Travis finished her sentence. "Got her permission," he muttered drowsily against the back of Melissa's head as he fitted his naked body to hers and wrapped a possessive arm around her waist. "Go back to sleep. Elaine's taken over." He nestled his head on the pillow beside hers and relaxed into instant slumber.

There was no more protests from the woman he held in his arms. Travis's deep, even breathing was strangely relaxing to Melissa. Somehow it just made sense that he should be sleeping in her bed with his arms around her. Drifting back into the dream she'd been having when Travis joined her, it didn't seem peculiar at all that her mother had given Travis permission to sleep with her daughter.

Chain saws droned and whined throughout most of the day but the sound was only a faint buzzing filtering through the dreams of the couple lying nestled close together beneath the covers. They weren't aware of the many rings of the telephone, nor the stream of people who came and went on Wintersfield throughout the daylight hours. By nightfall, the farm was quiet, the darkness shrouding the empty places where buildings and stately trees should have stood.

The deep rumble of a bullfrog sounded in the distance, crickets sang from the fields, and fireflies flickered their golden lanterns as they flitted here and there. One room in the small rambler shone with light, and the faint sounds of a television program filtered through the screens that covered the

window and door. They were the normal sounds
and lights of a typical summer evening except there
were none coming from the sprawling old farmhouse.

Melissa stirred slightly and came awake slowly.
When she opened her eyes and encountered darkness, years of habit instructed her that it was the
predawn hours and that she must roll out of bed and
start the morning chores. Unmindful of anything
beyond that, she prepared to get up until she realized she was being held in place. Travis! He really
was in bed with her!

"Don't move," was the softly spoken order growled
from somewhere just beyond her ear.

The hours of sleep had restored some of Melissa's
strength and rejuvenated her will. "You can't order
me around," she muttered as she started to roll toward the edge of the bed.

Travis tightened his grip and slid his other arm
around her, the twin action effectively keeping her
still. "I will only when I have to, and this is one of
those times."

His voice was still husky with sleep, but there was
no sign of Morpheus-induced weakness in the arms
that hauled her back against him. "Lissa, Lissa,
you're the most comfortable woman to sleep with.
So soft," he judged as he kissed her shoulder, then
began to nuzzle along its smooth curve.

"I'm sure you've known many," Melissa mocked
as she tried to squirm away from the tantalizing
kisses he was pressing on her neck. A delicious lan-
guour stole through her limbs, and a warmth built
deep inside her.

"A few," he murmured as he flicked the tip of his tongue against her earlobe. "No one I wanted to hold all night and every night, though. None of them made such a nice pillow."

The weight of his head was heavy on her breasts, and she became indignant when his fingers gently pushed against the soft twin curves as if to increase his own comfort. He sprawled across the length of her, his hair-roughened thigh thrown over her stomach. His breath was soft and steady at her bosom, telling her he was now sleeping again. Having adjusted his pillow more properly, Travis was settled in for the duration.

For a few moments, Melissa contemplated the role Travis had assigned her. Being considered an adequate headrest didn't do much for her ego or her breathing. She could barely inhale. She twisted beneath him, becoming increasingly frustrated as his slumbering form allowed for her restless movements by rearranging itself. His thigh slid off her stomach and between her legs, his head moved to the crook of her neck, and his arms thrust beneath her pillow. Melissa no longer served as just a soft support for his head—but had become his unwilling mattress.

"Travis!" She grabbed hold of a lock of his hair and tugged hard.

"Hey!" Travis woke with a start. He lifted his head and found himself staring into a pair of rebellious blue eyes. For a moment or two he was disoriented, but then he felt the silken mutiny taking place in the soft feminine body underneath him. Although he hadn't attained his full requirement of sleep, he couldn't help but enjoy the lush attack of two quivering breasts into his chest, the thrust of a female pelvis against his hips and the agitated stroking of warm bare toes along his calves.

"If you're feeling that frisky, I'll be happy to oblige." He grinned, languidly, his lashes lifting fractionally. "But I thought we could both use a few more hours of rest."

"Oh!" she gasped and froze all movement. "Get off of me," she pleaded. "I can't breathe." She gave him a weak shove.

"Lissa, have a heart," he moaned. "All I want to do is sleep with you. I've dreamed about this for weeks." He had the good grace to slide at least partway off her but retained his grasp around her. "Just let me hold you. Be happy with that for a little while longer. Later, I promise," he muttered into the pillow as his hands slithered up her rib cage and cupped her breasts.

She lay still. Travis's breath was warm and caressing across her cheek. A tendril of her hair lifted and dropped hypnotically with each of his inhalations and exhalations. Melissa wasn't as wide awake as she had thought. In a few more minutes, she gave up the battle and fell back asleep.

SHE WAS IN A BOAT bobbing gently up and down on a quiet sea. Her cheek lay against the smooth deck, her hand open on an oddly textured surface. But before she could assimilate the feeling, her hand was being guided along an unfamiliar course. At the same time, she felt the deck heave beneath her and a grating roughness along her jaw.

Melissa opened her eyes. This was no boat and

there was no quiet sea. Her upper body lay across Travis Winters's chest. The bucking motion had been his means of moving her legs off his. The grating roughness was the rasp of his beard against her skin. Even as she digested the information, she was aware that he had hold of her hand. She hoped he didn't feel her sharp intake of breath when he guided her palm to his bold arousal.

She shut her eyes as an explosion of desire went off inside her at the sound of his muted groan. Was he still asleep? Was she a part of some dream? Or was he aware of what he was doing? She kept her eyes firmly closed.

It was a delicious sensation to be the cause of his obvious excitement, whether it was unconscious or not. She would lie very still until she knew for certain he was awake, then let him know he'd overstepped his bounds. In the meantime, it wouldn't hurt to punish him a little for treating her like an inanimate pillow. She would leave him in no doubt that she was a woman, then retreat before matters got completely out of hand.

She had missed him, and although she had too much pride to tell him just how much, she didn't intend to let this opportunity go by without getting something out of it for herself. It would feel so good to have him make love to her one last time. She only wished he loved her, and not just what she represented to him.

She was hearth and home, a pair of warm slippers on a cold night. He didn't want her because she was the most desirable creature he'd ever laid eyes on, but because she was so *comfortable*. She felt sad that as a little boy he'd probably never owned a teddy bear, but she couldn't be that for him, she had to be more. Maybe now was her chance to show him that she wasn't a security blanket, but a seductive woman.

She gave a soft sigh that she hoped he would think came from the depths of a sound slumber. She allowed her fingers to flutter over the crisp wedge of hair that surrounded the seat of his passion. With a tiny thrill of female satisfaction, she felt the instant contraction of muscle in his flat belly. Deliberately she gave the impression that she was restless in sleep, involved in some sexual fantasy that definitely had a man involved but not necessarily the man writhing beneath her teasing touch.

Her feigned restlessness included a provocative brush of her breasts across his turgid nipples. "Oh God," she heard him whisper, and to her everlasting shame, she couldn't prevent a betraying giggle.

The next second she was flat on her back and Travis was the one on top. Keeping her hands trapped between their bodies, still in intimate contact with him, he stared down into her flushed face. "Enjoying yourself?" he questioned, his eyes more gold than brown.

"I...I...." She couldn't think of a thing to say that wouldn't sound totally idiotic. Crying foul wouldn't appease him, nor would a plea of temporary insanity even though the slow rhythmic movements of his hips were driving her out of her mind.

"I am, too," he drawled thickly as if responding to what he thought she'd been trying to say. He closed his hand over one breast, his fingers a warm brand against her skin. "I can't get this kind of service in the jungle," he teased, but he was the one providing the service. He eased a tight nipple into his mouth and licked the surrounding flesh with the tip of his tongue.

Her moans were at least as anguished as his had been when she'd been the one doing the teasing. His fingers and mouth were an endless torment, renewing a search begun months before and probing ever closer to the treasure he sought. When he delved deeply for the feminine riches secreted inside her body, she was more than ready to relinquish them into his possession. Half-crazed with need, she realized the only way she would gain relief was to begin her own treasure hunt.

"Lissa!" His strangled exclamation followed the renewed movement of her hands between his thighs. "Oh yes!" he groaned. "Now...please," he gasped, and Melissa was entirely willing to comply.

She guided him to her but it was Travis's driving thrust that completed their union. Melissa met the sheer power in him, the unleashed hunger in his forceful lovemaking, and they moved at an exhilarating pace. Two months' frustration was released with their coming together. Two months of need were erased in a matter of minutes as they met at the apex of joy and melded into one glorious entity.

As one they partook of the highest pleasure, savored every facet of it until they were replete. It took a long time for them to recover, both overwhelmed by their own feelings. Travis was the first to speak, and there was a funny catch in his voice. "We digressed from the rules a bit, didn't we?"

"Rules?" Melissa had no idea what he was talking about. She was too busy trying to rally the defenses that had deserted her right along with her common sense. Now, she was at a disadvantage.

If the statement he'd made yesterday about buying Gus out was any indication, he intended to commandeer both Wintersfield and her. He'd already requisitioned the latter and encountered little resistance. She knew he would next seize the farm. Travis might not like to think he had anything of his father in him, but he had all the makings of a first-rate military commander. Perry's historic quote came to mind and she mentally paraphrased it to size up the situation she now found herself in: *I have met the enemy and she is mine.*

"Don't you remember?" He propped himself up on one elbow so he could look into her face. "First we were supposed to share a hello kiss." He paused to consider something, then shrugged. "I guess one could say we fulfilled that requirement."

Taking a strand of her hair, he wrapped it securely around his wrist. "Then, we were supposed to exchange a friendly greeting." He extended that courtesy. "Good morning, my love."

Travis was absolutely thunderstruck when Melissa promptly dissolved into tears.

11

"What the...?" Travis asked, completely dumb-founded. "Why are you crying?" He took hold of Melissa's shoulders anxiously. "I didn't hurt you, did I?"

She shook her head, but the tears continued to spill like rivers down her cheeks. Her fingers clutched the snowy sheets, pulling them up to hide her nakedness.

"We just made glorious, wonderful love and you're crying about it?"

"Yes, I'm crying about it," she cried. "I didn't want to make love with you."

Once, not too long ago, Travis would have reacted to that kind of statement by withdrawing, but now he knew that they needed to be together and he was determined to make her see that. Maybe he was bull-dozing her, but she was too important to him to slip through his fingers again. Months in the jungle had shown him that his life was worth nothing without her. Her call had proven she needed him, too.

Melissa had been through a great deal, and per-haps he was going too fast, but Travis didn't know any other way. They'd wasted too much time al-ready—time when they could have been together. "Of course you wanted to make love with me," he soothed. "You love me, honey."

Melissa searched his face, knowing there was no way she could deny his words. There was not an ounce of doubt in his eyes. She was lost—couldn't even salvage her pride. Mustering all her dignity, she strove for some measure of control. "Well that's *my* problem, not yours."

He shifted his weight and looked at her quizzically. "Problem? I don't see it as a problem."

"Of course you don't!" The tears fell faster. "You're not the one doing the loving!"

"Who says?" His eyes danced with amusement.

Melissa sat up in the bed, striving for a more advantageous position. She saw no sense in trying to leave because he would just pull her back down again. But the rigidity in her body let him know she was staying under protest. Although she was not as strong as he was, she'd had enough of his high-handedness. She might not be able to get past her admission of love, but she wasn't going to let him use it against her. Before she'd let that happen, she'd pack her bags and take Kenny and herself off to someplace where Travis would never find them.

"*I* say," she managed doggedly. "You come charging in here like the cavalry to the rescue, but I'm not some helpless damsel in distress. I may love you, Travis Winters, but I'm not going to lie down and let you walk all over me!"

His laugh was both amused and provoking. "That's not what I've been doing to you and we both know it. As I recall, I was the one lying down and your fingers were doing all the walking."

"Liar! You were awake every minute and you started it!" How dare he suggest that *she* had taken advantage of *him*. The man was more than a cad. He was literally rubbing her nose in her own weakness.

"Oh no," he declared firmly, grabbing hold of her hair and pulling her face down to his. "I'm not letting you get off the right subject. Who started our lovemaking is completely irrelevant. The point is, that it was just that! Making love."

Her eyes blazed into his, refusing to back down. It didn't matter that she was sprawled over him without a stitch on, that her breasts were flattened against his chest and her bare legs entangled with his. She was fighting for her principles and she was immune to everything else. "Don't glorify it! We had sex, pure and simple!"

It didn't take Melissa long to realize she had gone too far. Travis's mouth hardened. The gold lights went off in his eyes. "Listen," he said fiercely. "I didn't ride a damned jeep through miles of jungle in the middle of the night, spend two days running through airports just to have sex with you! I can get that anywhere!"

Travis felt her quiver beneath the force of his words and was filled with a grim satisfaction. When he was done with her, she'd never do this to him again.

He flipped her over on the mattress and came down on top of her. "You are going to listen to me and take back every rotten thing you've said. I love you, Melissa Lindstrand, and I've never said that to another living soul." His voice rose higher. "Not another soul! Do you hear me!"

"The whole world can hear... what did you say?"

"Humph!" he exclaimed disgustedly. "Am I finally getting through to you?"

Melissa gaped at him, her heart pounding heavily in her chest. "You . . . you just said you love me," she said wonderingly.

"Damned right I did," he agreed. At last! At last she understood what he'd been trying to tell her from almost the beginning of their relationship. Even if he'd spoken the words in anger, he'd finally found the guts to say them. Last time he was with her, he hadn't know how to express what he felt. He had mistakenly assumed that she knew he loved her.

After all, she'd been through this love business before, spent her whole life in a loving atmosphere. He was the novice and had needed her to guide him along. His tone was slightly accusing. "I have been telling you that I love you every way I know how since I came back. I might even have loved you when I left, but you didn't give me any encouragement."

The delight in her eyes belied her defensive statement. "You could have told me that, you know. I can't read your mind, Travis."

Taking a deep sigh, he rolled away from her and stared up at the ceiling. His anger was gone, replaced by a wary resignation. Even now he wasn't ready to verbalize the full extent of his feelings. His insides still felt raw. He had given her the words, what more did she want? "I was hoping you could. It sure would've made things a helluva lot easier on me. I . . . uh . . . I need a cigarette." He rolled to the edge of the mattress and started to swing his legs over the side.

"Oh, no you don't," Melissa said as she wrapped her arms around him. "You'd better keep talking. There are ways of breaking the most stubborn of men." Her fingers trailed lower and soon they weren't talking at all.

A LONG TIME LATER Melissa opened her eyes and grinned. "Now, about all these feelings you've been having...?"

"Go easy with me, you amazon," he begged in mock fear. He shrank backward, his shoulder blades cowering against her breasts. A loud growl erupted in his stomach. "I'm too weak to fight you. You've drained me of my vital essences and I'm half-starved," he whined pathetically. "I don't suppose you could see your way clear to feeding me a scrap or two before continuing the torture."

The last thing Melissa had had on her mind was food until Travis brought up the subject. She hadn't eaten since the previous morning and was definitely feeling hollow. She considered his suggestion for a moment, her fingers drumming impatiently in the vicinity of his navel. When she finally decided a meal was in order, it was almost too late. "No one can accuse me of being a cruel warden. Let's adjourn to the kitchen."

Travis batted her hand away from him. "And that's not cruel?" he asked. "Look what you've already done to me." He slipped out of bed and stood up, letting her see the result of her touch.

With a feline smile, she twirled a strand of hair around her finger. "Then again, I might be persuaded to postpone breakfast."

"Oh no," he negated far more quickly than she would've liked. Reaching down, he hauled her out of bed. "We've done more than enough lollygagging already. I learned that lesson the last time I was here. Never let it be said that Travis Winters has lost sight of the practical."

Yesterday, when he'd told her he had to do a few errands before coming to bed, he must have gone back to his car for his luggage. A large duffle bag was propped near the door. Travis pulled out a shaving kit and unmindful of his nakedness opened the door. "Get a move on, Lissa. we can't spend all day talking. There's too much work to be done."

Melissa knew that he was retaliating for the treatment she'd once given him, but she still couldn't help feeling a twinge of annoyance. How could he stand there tantalizing her with his naked glory and telling her they had work to do?

In the following half hour she learned that the practical side of his nature was easily as strong as her own. Taking a shower together could have been a romantic interlude, and she had hoped it would be, but it was hardly that. All he did was remind her of his hunger and urge her to hurry as he scrubbed his body. She didn't rinse the soap out of her hair fast enough to suit him and he took over the task himself, holding her head under the spray until she thought she might drown. She was feeling very disgruntled when he filled the sink in order to shave, and he didn't respond well at all when she slipped her arms around his waist and pressed herself against his clean, damp body.

"Let's move, Lissa," he commanded her reflection in the mirror. "You get dressed and start breakfast. I'll be down shortly."

By the time he came downstairs to the kitchen, the

food was on the table. Once she set her mind to it, she was nothing if not efficient. As he slid into the place set for him, Melissa noted they were wearing similar clothes, blue jeans and chambray shirts. Their brown leather boots were almost identical. "Dressed for the part, I see," she commented as she placed a plate of bacon and eggs in front of him.

She was surprised at his reaction to her words. "I'm not playing a part, Lissa. I thought I'd convinced you of that already."

She held up her hand, touched by his defensiveness. Her love for him shone in her eyes. "I was just teasing."

He picked up his fork and lowered his head, hiding his expression. "I think I've got quite a bit to learn. I hope you have lots of patience, Lissa."

"Oh, I think I do," she assured. Knowing he loved her would give her enough patience for both of them.

Travis liked that answer. If he played his cards right, he might not ever have to bare his soul. There was something about opening himself up completely that scared him. He knew she loved him, wanted him, but would she still feel that way when she realized he wasn't nearly as strong as he pretended? If things worked out—and he would do his best to make sure they did—he would have a wedding band on her finger before she found out what a coward he was.

"I even have the patience to wait until after breakfast for you to tell me when you first discovered that you loved me."

Travis didn't meet her eyes and addressed himself

totally to his food, wolfing down eggs as fast as he could. If she had asked him to jump off a bridge for her he would have done it in a second, but the thought of verbalizing his feelings terrified him. Maybe he could manage to get her to put his emotions into words, and he'd nod his head in all the appropriate places. He didn't feel the need for further discussion, but she evidently wanted a full disclosure.

Until he'd met Melissa, he hadn't been aware that he had these soggy, sentimental kinds of feelings. Now that she had found out that he did, she was determined to dissect them with a fine-toothed comb. Admitting to himself that he was a dull lovesick fool was one thing, but did she have to expose him like this? She wanted a pound of his flesh but he wasn't going to give it up without a fight. A man had to have some pride.

Melissa made no comment as she watched him shovel down the food. They had gone without eating for too long, and the next minutes were used to fill their empty stomachs. The only conversation between them was confined to passing second helpings and asking for the salt and pepper. Finally Melissa had satisfied her hunger. She brought the coffeepot to the table.

"Before talking about anything else, there's something that has really been bothering me," Melissa admitted. "Did you really get my mother's permission to sleep with me?"

"Don't worry," he said smugly. "She's read the *Farmer's Almanac*." As if that answer should have satisfied her curiosity, he went on drinking his coffee. He reached for the last piece of toast and slathered it with strawberry jam. His eyes lingered hungrily on her passion-bruised lips. "This will have to do until I can get at the real thing."

Melissa was not about to be side-tracked. She couldn't understand how her straitlaced mother could have condoned their intimacy, or why this year's weather forecasts should have anything to do with the matter. "Will you kindly stop filling your face and tell me what the *Almanac* has to do with us?"

"For a farmer, you sure don't keep up on things, do you? I would've thought you read that thing from cover to cover." He nonchalantly continued munching his toast, but there was a devilish twinkle in his dark eyes.

"I have read it from cover to cover, and there was nothing about us in it. If you could rely on the thing, I would have known the storm was coming. It predicted balmy weather."

"The forecasts might be a bit too general," he agreed as he licked jam from his fingers. "But you can't deny the state law." He quoted verbatim from a "supposed" Minnesota statute. "When in the presence of a girl's mother and father, it is considered a legal proposal of marriage to do any of the following: hug the girl; kiss the girl; or present her with a box of candy. I plead guilty to the first and have agreed for the ceremony to take place some time next week."

"What?" Melissa couldn't believe her own ears.

"When I first met you, I thought you were a bit slow and you've given me little reason to change that opinion." He spied a copy of the latest edition on the kitchen counter and within seconds had found the law in question. Coming back to the table, he placed the book down in front of her and pointed to the passage. "It's all there in black and white. I'm a law-abiding man, and I don't want to make any trouble."

She couldn't help but laugh when she read the entry describing the remote out-of-date statute that still remained on the law books, but she wasn't going to let him get away with such nonsense. "If this is your idea of a proposal, Travis, it lacks a certain romance. You've taken practicality a step too far and I'm not impressed." She picked up a cold piece of bacon and began munching on it.

Swiftly he took a glance out of the kitchen window. She was getting that inquisitorial look in her eyes again. "A man's got to do what a man's got to do," he quipped. "And right now, this man's got a lot of work waiting for him. We'll discuss our upcoming marriage later. I have to go see a man about a new barn, and I think your mom and dad just pulled in."

He ignored her outraged expression and strode briskly to the door. With one hand on the doorknob, he seemed to change his mind and came back to her. He gave her a hurried peck on the cheek. "Don't dawdle over your food, honey. Your little boy's home, and you're supposed to set a good example."

"Kenny?" Things were happening so fast she couldn't keep up with him. "He's at my brother's."

"Your folks picked him up this morning," Travis called over his shoulder as he walked back to the door. "Elaine and I decided that you needed him here. He's only five, Lissa. He needs his mother. Take it easy today and spend some time with your son." He pulled open the screen door. "See you later."

He had always been cocky, but now that he was sure of her feelings, the annoying trait had reached mammoth proportions. She'd be subjected to these kinds of orders for the rest of her life if she agreed to his ridiculous proposal. As she started clearing up the breakfast dishes, she admitted that she'd probably enjoy it. Travis had his vulnerable side but didn't like to show it. She knew there was a disgustingly lovesick look on her face as she gazed out the kitchen window and watched him saunter down the drive. Too bad he was so damned sexy!

In the upcoming years she was going to let him get away with murder. Look what had happened over breakfast. He had promised that he would talk to her. She wanted answers to all the questions women had before they were satisfied with a man's affection. When was the exact moment he knew he loved her? She wanted details. What did he love the most about her? Did all other women pale in comparison to her? Had he pined away for her the whole time he was off in South America? These and other burning issues needed to be resolved in the immediate future! She'd let him off the hook this morning, but there wouldn't be a bride at this hasty put-up job of a wedding if she didn't get some answers!

Kenny entered the kitchen on a run. "Hi, mom," he yelled loudly, caught sight of her by the sink, then launched himself across the room and into her arms. His tight hug was heartfelt but brief. "Can I go with Travis, mom? Can I?"

"You just got home, champ." Melissa arched a questioning brow at her mother who was stepping inside from the porch. "I thought you and Travis had decided Kenny needed to be with me. What's going on?"

Kenny took her question as his answer, and his face fell. "But he's going to a computer place. He needs me, mom. We're going to have the best barn ever, and I get to help decide on stuff."

"At least one of us is being consulted," Melissa muttered caustically. "A computer place, huh?" She recalled an earlier conversation when Travis had brought up the subject of computers and shook her head. She glanced beseechingly at her mother. "Does he have *any* idea how much that kind of thing will cost?"

"I'm sure this is only the initial investigation," Elaine placated, her shrewd eyes probing her daughter's face for clues that would provide her with answers to an entirely different set of questions. "Kenny wants to go, dear. You and I have a lot to talk about, and that won't be any fun for Kenny. I don't see any harm in it."

Melissa rolled her eyes heavenward, then ruffled her son's hair. "Looks like I'm outnumbered." Over the top of Kenny's head, she cast Elaine a quelling glance. "And there *are* a few things I'd like to discuss with your grandmother."

"Thanks, mom," Kenny declared happily, and raced for the door. "See you later."

"Mmm," Melissa confirmed, but her son was already outside and racing toward Gus's place. "If I didn't know better, I'd say there's something about me that drives the male of the species away. Kenny's the second one to run out on me this morning."

"At least Kenny seems more happy about it. Travis looked like he was being chased by demons. He stopped long enough to ask Kenny if he wanted to go into town with him, then took off down the driveway." Elaine turned away from Melissa to reach for a cup. After pouring herself some coffee, she inquired, "What did you do to him anyway?"

"What did *I* do to *him?*" Melissa scoffed incredulously. "Let's get our facts straight, shall we? According to Travis, the two of you have already arranged for our wedding. I'm the one being railroaded here, wouldn't you say?"

Elaine's beaming smile forecast her opinion as accurately as the words that followed. "I think it's wonderful. I just love a man who rushes in and sweeps a girl off her feet."

"A girl or her mother?" Melissa questioned as she took the kitchen chair opposite Elaine's. She knew she'd never convince her mother that wedding plans should at least be initiated by the bride, so didn't even try.

For the next hour they talked about Travis and the upcoming marriage. Eventually Melissa accepted that in one short week, she was going to have a brand-new husband and Kenny a father. As they continued to converse, Melissa found herself more and more amazed at her mother's perceptiveness. Everything she said about Travis made complete sense.

"I haven't been married to your father for over thirty years and raised three sons without learning something about men," Elaine stated after her daughter had asked how she'd reached the conclusion that Travis was running scared. "He thinks he's already wearing his heart on his sleeve and can't understand why you won't settle for that."

Melissa thought that over for several moments and finally concluded that her mother could be right. Travis had been avoiding further questions ever since he'd told her that he loved her. "But that's so silly. I'm not asking for the moon—just the usual things a woman wants to know from the man she loves. Like when did he find out that he loves me. Gordy told me everything I wanted to know before we were married."

"This man isn't like Gordy, though, is he? And the truth is, you don't want him to be. Gordy was a good man, but he didn't suit you. You've had to carry too much for too long, Melissa. Now you have a partner—a man— to help you."

"Travis is that all right," agreed Melissa. "Even so, it would be nice to know how this miracle happened."

"It took me ten years to get that kind of information out of your father." Elaine's voice softened with the memory. "Patience is a virtue," she advised. "Let Travis explain himself to you in his own good time, and you'll never regret it."

Melissa was astounded when her mother emitted the tinkling laughter of an accomplished coquette. She didn't know why she was so surprised. Her mother couldn't have become a successful match-maker without being thoroughly familiar with the complexities of men. "So you think I should let Travis get away with all this?" she asked. "Not ask any questions and let nature take its course?"

"If it already hasn't," Elaine concluded knowingly.

"Mother!" To her dying day, she'd never get over the last twenty-four hours. Her whole life had been turned upside down—and her own mother not only approved but had assisted Travis to bring it about! "You're really something. You know that?"

"Of course, dear." Elaine smiled. "How else could I have given birth to such a fine daughter? Now, let's get to work. I never said Travis has to have everything his own way. We women can offer a few surprises of our own."

TRAVIS'S "SURPRISE" STOOD ADMIRING HERSELF in the mirror attached to her bedroom door. Melissa looked nothing like her usual self in the teal silk dress that was glamorous, backless and a bit racy. She had purchased it during a mad fling in a downtown boutique on a day when she'd felt particularily low and decidedly unfeminine. She'd never worn it and was slightly amazed with herself for having the courage to try it out on Travis.

The silver short-sleeved silk jacket provided some security, for the bodice was cut low and only a slender band of silk around her neck held it up. The tulip hem gave a provocative glimpse of her thigh, and her sheer hose added an intriguing shimmer to her long legs. Her satin sandals were set on high slender heels that made her legs seem even longer. A smoky shade of eye shadow added mystery to her eyes, dark mascara enhanced her lashes, and a touch of blusher and lipstick lent the finishing touches to her face. She was going to knock Travis's socks off!

There was a rap on her bedroom door, and she pulled it open. Elaine bustled into the room, her face wearing a self-satisfied expression. "Kenny thinks you look like a fairy princess, but I made him promise not to say a word to Travis."

She gave Melissa a once-over with her eyes. "You should wear your hair up more often. It shows off your neck and pretty ears. Grandma's pearl studs are perfect. You really do look regal, sweetheart."

"Thank you." Melissa lifted her hand to the exposed skin at her nape. She'd pulled her long hair into a high French twist, then curled the loose strands that fell over her forehead and ears. "I hope Travis likes it."

"He will," Elaine stated with certainty. "Kenny's already out in the car with your father, so I guess it's time for me to go. Don't worry about him. We're picking up Teddy on the way home, and you know how well those boys get along."

"I still feel a little guilty over this. I haven't been with Kenny since the storm."

"Kenny will be fine," Elaine judged firmly. "You just go out and have a nice time. Both you and Travis deserve it. Gus thought it was a great idea. Once again, you're outnumbered, my girl."

"So I am." Melissa smiled as she followed her mother down the stairs.

TRAVIS NEVER TOOK HIS EYES OFF MELISSA, not even when the steward asked him his preference in wine. He reeled off the name of some expensive vintage and sent the man on his way. "I can't get over it," he murmured dazedly, his eyes so intensely gold that Melissa blushed whenever she met his gaze.

"Get over what?" she asked as she studied the large brocade-edged menu.

"How well you clean up," Travis got out through the tightness in his throat.

"Thank you, kind sir." Melissa didn't fish for a more flowery compliment. The stunned and yearning look on Travis's face hadn't changed from the moment he'd come to pick her up. He made her feel beautiful, the most desirable creature on earth, and her inner happiness shone like brilliant stars in her blue eyes. She wanted to return the favor. "You look very handsome and distinguished yourself. I like seeing you in a suit. That light brown shows off your gorgeous hair and eyes."

"A man can wear his blue suit or his brown suit but that dress is—" He took a swipe at the lock dipping over his forehead. "I could undress you with one finger...I could...." He let out his breath. "I think the rest of my thoughts are illegal."

When a small measure of wine was poured for Travis to test, he swallowed it quickly, then asked for a full glass and drained it in three swallows. "It's fine," he pronounced, without having even tasted it.

The wine steward was accustomed to patrons who showed little finesse with their selections, but he'd been almost positive that this man was a connoisseur of fine wine. The vintage he had chosen was not usually ordered by someone who intended to gulp it down like soda pop. "Very good, sir," he forced out before leaving the table, not quite able to hide the sarcastic edge to his voice.

Melissa hid her amused smile behind her napkin. Travis hadn't even noticed the steward's displeasure. "Isn't this a lovely restaurant, Travis? This hotel has always enjoyed a five-star rating." She hoped some casual conversation would relieve the almost overwhelming sexual tension between them.

Although she was gratified by Travis's reaction to her plans for the evening, it was somewhat disconcerting to feel that she was the most delectable item on tonight's menu. "Travis?" she repeated when he didn't answer her, his golden eyes devouring the bare skin of her shoulders and silk-covered bosom. Maybe she should have left her jacket on until she'd sprung her last surprise and led him upstairs to the room she'd reserved on the twenty-third floor.

He seemed to be struggling with some obstruction in his throat when he finally realized she had asked him a question. "Did you say something?"

It was difficult, but she managed to divert his attention from her long enough to enjoy dinner. At least, she enjoyed hers. Travis showed a decided lack of interest in his prime rib even though it was done to perfection. He passed on the after-dinner drinks, and when she asked him to take her out on the dance floor, he looked as if she was punishing him for some heinous crime.

"I hope I can get through this," he grumbled as he took hold of her arm and guided her onto the parqueted floor.

"Don't you like to dance?" She loved to dance and

had been looking forward to this part of the evening. She'd chosen this restaurant with after-dinner dancing in mind.

Travis pulled her into his arms and held her so closely she could barely breathe. He was an excellent dancer, but his mind wasn't on the movements of his feet. Eventually, as they swayed together to the slow music he came to a complete halt in the middle of the dance floor. He stared deeply into her eyes. "What would happen if I took a room here for the night?" he murmured hopefully.

"The room I reserved would go to waste," she whispered back.

Travis gaped at her until they drew the curious stares of several other couples on the dance floor. "Waste not, want not, and do I ever want you," he groaned, softly.

"My sentiments, exactly," Melissa said as she propelled him off the floor, out of the restaurant and to the elevators in the lobby.

"Since after tonight, you'll have completely compromised my virtue," Travis began as soon as they were inside the elevator, "don't you think you'd better marry me?"

Melissa, who had been twirling the hotel key around her finger, lost all her poise. An elderly couple, who had been standing quietly to one side, turned to stare at her. The man had a noticeable twinkle in his eye as he said, "That's right young fella. A man's got to protect his reputation. If her intentions aren't honorable, don't go with her. My mother almost had to shove this woman down the aisle with a shotgun to get her to marry me."

The plump, white-haired woman had her own

advice to offer. "Don't listen to him, my dear. If you don't show them how you mean to go while they're young, they'll take complete advantage of you. Your young man is quite good-looking but that's not everything. Can he cook? Don't offer him a proposal until you find out if he keeps a clean house."

By the time Travis and Melissa had escaped the elevator, Travis was sorry he'd ever opened his mouth. "Could you believe that woman? I bet she leads that poor man around by the nose."

"According to my stock manual, that's the only way to handle a good bull." Melissa unlocked the door to their room. With a lascivious smile on her face, she struck a provocative pose against the door and crooked her finger at Travis. "Aren't you coming inside?"

The gold glimmers in his eyes were tinged with caution as he contemplated her question. "You haven't assigned me with a number, have you?" he queried suspiciously as he edged around her resplendent form. "After you've placed your ring in my nose, I won't become just another number in your stock manual?"

"You're number one in my stock manual, Travis. There won't be any other entries." She reached for the fragile fastening at her neck. "And the only ring I want is the one that goes on my finger."

Sometime later, in the wee hours of the morning, Melissa raised up on one elbow, looking tenderly at the sleeping man who, during the last few hours, had affirmed his love for her in countless ways. The tremors of power and love that had shuddered through him as he'd laid claim to her body meant more to her than any words he could have spoken. The words would come later, in the next few weeks, or months or years. It really didn't matter to her.

With a secret smile on her face, she snuggled against him and he immediately drew her closer into the shelter of his strong arms. Until Travis was ready to open himself up to her, she would just have to settle for innumerable times like this. She gave a soft contented sigh and admitted to herself that her mother was indeed a very wise woman. Patience *was* a virtue.

The Fourth
Harlequin American Romance
Premier Edition

GENTLY INTO NIGHT
KATHERINE COFFARO

Emily Ruska and Joel Kline
are two New York City police detectives
caught between conflicting values
and an undeniable attraction
for each other.

Harlequin Intrigue

Because romance can be quite an adventure

Exclusive Harlequin home subscriber benefits!
- •SPECIAL LOW PRICES for home subscribers only
- •CONVENIENCE of home delivery
- •NO CHARGE for postage and handling
- •FREE *Harlequin Romance Digest*®
- •FREE BONUS books
- •NEW TITLES 2 months ahead of retail
- •MEMBER of the largest romance fiction book club in the world